Doctor Who – Full Circle

DOCTOR WHO
FULL CIRCLE

Based on the BBC television serial by Andrew Smith by
arrangement with the British Broadcasting Corporation

ANDREW SMITH

A TARGET BOOK
published by
the Paperback Division of
W. H. Allen & Co. Ltd.

A Target Book
Published in 1982
by the Paperback Division of W. H. Allen & Co. Ltd
A Howard & Wyndham Company
44 Hill Street, London W1X 8LB

Reprinted 1983

First published in Great Britain by
W. H. Allen & Co. Ltd 1982

Typeset by V & M Graphics Ltd, Aylesbury, Bucks
Printed in Great Britain by The Anchor Press Ltd, Tiptree, Essex

ISBN 0 426 20150 7

To the cast, crew and production team of the television production *Full Circle*. Thank you.

Contents

Prologue

I

Twisting, burning metal screamed at a pitch which challenged the death-yells of the passengers and crew members throughout the massive structure of the starliner as the great space vessel hurtled, out of control, towards the shifting grey mists that enshrouded the surface of the terror planet Alzarius.

Those in areas of the ship where the meteors had damaged the hull insulation died burning, horrible deaths, their corpses dragged out into space to fall towards the planet in the starliner's wake.

On the bridge, ashen-faced Commander Yakob Lorenzil ignored a severe gash in his left arm to view on the master monitor high on the wall before him the mists of Alzarius through which the starliner now cut a red, blazing path.

Aware again of the intolerable heat, and of the pain his arm, Lorenzil clutched at his wound and let himself fall back into his chair.

Sub-Commander Damyen Fenrik had taken the place of the dead Chief Pilot at the central flight console. Blinking the sweat from his eyes, he surveyed the instruments before him with giddy terror, the beat of his own heart pulsing achingly in his ears.

'Impact imminent!' he cried.

Lorenzil yelled, 'Ready yourselves!' and with his good hand secured the double clasp of his chair harness. He wondered if it would be strong enough to hold him. What would happen if –?

On the master monitor the treetops of an Alzarian forest were visible for one split instant and then the universe exploded inside Lorenzil's head.

The starliner landed hot and heavy on the forest, tearing a huge, burning portion of it away from the surface of the planet.

The noise – greater, he was sure, than any noise that had ever existed in the history of creation – blotted from Lorenzil's mind his thoughts of how many of his crew and passengers were dying in that instant.

The blackness came and Lorenzil's last thoughts in life were that he was going to survive the crash after all.

Fenrik had not expected that his first command would be over what was little more than a scorched chunk of metal. By Terradonian law he was now Commander-Designate of the starliner, but there was no doubting that the shop would never fly again – in his lifetime, at least. In their efforts to evade the meteor cluster the Terradonian space craft had veered wildly from its projected flight path. There was little hope of rescue. Few people ever dared venture to Alzarius.

Fenrik patrolled the ship dutifully, exchanging words with terrified engineers, anxious technicians and – when he could spare the time – the occasional wounded passenger or crewman.

There was a second, slightly less immediate, cause for concern among the crew and passengers who still lived – less immediate, but more frightening than any concerns over food and water supply and the like.

This was Alzarius itself – the fog planet, home of how many unimaginable horrors? No one knew because no one had ever lived to describe them.

Fenrik tried to remember everything he knew of Alzarius. The mists came in cycles of some fifty years or so. And with the mists came death for any living being on the planet. Governmental and academic survey teams had at one time been despatched to Alzarius with great regularity, but not any more, for not one of those groups had ever been seen or heard of again. Unmanned satellites sent back pictures of their empty, lifeless space vessels sitting on the planet's surface, untended, in the process of decay. Any satellites sent in to land on Alzarius during the fog cycles had also been destroyed by whatever lurked under cover of the mists.

What chance did they have of surviving where no one else had managed to?

On the second day, an exploration team consisting of five volunteers was sent out. None of the five returned. The last contact with them was a radio distress call saying they were being attacked. Fenrik, listening to the call, thought he heard animal-like snarling behind the screams of the humans – then contact had been lost.

Fenrik lost another two teams within three days. At nightfall on their seventh day on Alzarius, he was called urgently to the ship's boarding area, where two men had been posted to watch for movement outside the vessel. One of them, Selman, was clearly very worried, clutching tensely at the knife from the kitchen galley with which he was armed.

'There's something out there, Mr Fenrik,' he stammered. 'Something ... I don't know.' The man was petrified, perspiring with fright.

Fenrik addressed Selman's companion. 'Huikson?'

The swarthy steward seemed unworried. 'We were standing outside there, sir.' He pointed to the sealed entrance door, a thick, heavy, impenetrable barrier. 'At the bottom of the ramp. Selman said he thought he saw or heard something ...'

'I saw them! Moving!' Selman cried. 'They're big ... I only glimpsed them, Mr Fenrik, but they're out there, I swear it, they're out there and they're coming to get us!'

'There's been no word from any of the watches posted by the hull ruptures,' said Fenrik. He recalled that Selman was – or had been on Terradon – a lawyer. Fenrik hated lawyers.

Huikson looked more than a little embarrassed. He tried to make excuses for Selman. 'The mist's getting thicker, sir. Drawing in a bit. Gets the imagination going. You know. Happens.'

They all heard the scraping sound on the other side of the entranceway.

9

Something was out there.

It came again. A hard, metallic grating sound.

When it came yet again there was obviously more than one of them.

Fenrik swore under his breath. He looked at Selman, saw him quivering and whimpering with fear, and inwardly damned the man for being right as he snatched down a wall radio and spoke into it. 'Commander Fenrik. Alert the ship – unidentified intruders are massing outside. Number unknown. Everyone is to be made ready to defend the starliner.'

The message went out over the passenger address system and everyone prepared themselves. There was not the level of panic that Fenrik might have feared – for many, this appeared to be a relief from all the tension and rumour of the past seven days. The enemy were here. They could at last do something concrete about dealing with that enemy.

Fenrik was joined in the boarding area by some thirty men carrying knives, tools, metal piping, anything that could be used as a weapon.

It seemed to have been a false alarm. The sounds from the door had stopped. For half an hour Fenrik and his men stood in total silence, save for the occasional reports coming in from the groups stationed by the hull ruptures. These reports stated that no movement outside the ship had been detected, no signs of life.

'Open the entrance.'

Fenrik's command prompted a number of uncertain, worried gazes from among the men around him. Then Huikson punched the appropriate sequence into a button panel by the door and the heavy portal started to rise up into the ceiling.

'They could still be out there, sir,' Huikson warned.

'I know,' Fenrik replied matter-of-factly, then moved towards the entrance. Dense, curling tongues of milky vapour lapped at him as he stepped out onto the shallow boarding ramp.

His men gathered behind him, infected by his courage, as Fenrik tried to peer out into the fog. It was futile. Visibility was down to six to eight feet.

Alzarius was silent.

They'll be back, Fenrik thought to himself as he turned to face the others.

'All right. Relax. There's nothing out there. Pass the word to the other –'

They appeared from nowhere, snarling and screaming, tall and hideous, dozens of them lumbering clumsily up the ramp.

Fenrik was the first to die, felled by a blow from a scaly, clawed hand.

In that same instant, hundreds more of the creatures began their attack on other vulnerable areas of the vessel.

The people of the starliner started the defence of their ship and of their lives.

It was to be a long and difficult battle.

II

When Mistfall comes
  The sun is swallowed whole
By sky-borne darkness
  The world turns to cold

When Mistfall comes
  The globe transforms its face
Grey fog clouds probe
  They reach to every place

When Mistfall comes
  The giants leave the swamp
The Marshmen walk the world
  The forestlands they haunt

When Mistfall comes
  The planet that has slept
Awakes, unleashing terror
  Bringing death if you forget

First Decider Yanek Pitrus,
Tenth generation starliner

'I Have Lost Control of the TARDIS'

A Time Lord summons cannot be ignored.

Romana repeated this to herself time and again, but it didn't help. The last thing she wanted was to return to her home planet of Gallifrey. She knew that if she did she would never again be able to experience the freedom she had so much enjoyed in the company of the Doctor.

The summons had been abrupt, explaining nothing. Romana sensed she knew the reason for it – at least in part. She was the reason. She felt this with a certainty that made her deeply melancholy.

It was not just freedom that the Doctor offered. It was adventure. It was wonderment. It was, ultimately, a new and deeper wisdom.

She watched him now as he manoeuvred a bewildering array of complicated instruments on one of the six facets of the TARDIS's main control console.

The Doctor and Romana had become very close in the time they had known one another, and yet he remained an enigma to her. Of one thing she was certain – he was not so confident and all-knowing as he frequently liked to suggest he was.

Would she see him again after Gallifrey? The face was at once immensely cheerful and yet tinged with the sadness of one who has known too many people for too short a time.

The lines on his face were deep, each one relating a story to her. She would miss him.

And K9, too. The computer constructed in the shape of a dog had accompanied her on a great many adventures. She had always found it very easy to think of K9 as more than a machine, rather as an individual, a friend.

'Are you ready, K9?' the Doctor wanted to know as he completed the preparatory adjustments of the control console.

'Master,' K9's shrill metallic voice confirmed.

'Right,' said the Doctor, crouching by the computer, 'I want you to set a course for binary co-ordinates ten zero eleven zero zero by zero two from galactic zero centre.'

The co-ordinates for Gallifrey! Romana turned away so that the Doctor would not see her lips tremble.

K9's antenna telescoped out towards the console. A moment passed, then, 'Co-ordinates laid in. Spatial drive initiated.' The console's central column began rising and falling, indicating they were in flight.

'Well done, K9,' said the Doctor. He looked vaguely in Romana's direction. 'Now we can be on our way.'

'You've made up your mind, then?'

The significance of her remark went straight past the Doctor. He rose, smiling, and headed for his coat and scarf on the nearby hatstand. 'You don't ignore a summons to Gallifrey.'

A Time Lord summons cannot be ignored.

As the Doctor clambered into his heavy burgundy coat, his back to Romana, he said enthusiastically, 'I'm looking forward to seeing how Leela and Andred are getting on. And you'll be able to meet your twin, K9.'

Leela was one of the Doctor's earlier companions, left behind on Gallifrey after a previous visit when she had fallen in love with Andred, a young Commander in the Chancellery Guard. K9's predecessor had been left with her for company.

Memories of Leela prompted a wide smile on the Doctor's face which faded as he turned and saw he was alone with K9 – the door to the corridor outside the control room stood ajar.

'Romana?' he called worriedly. When there was no reply he moved towards the door, draping his scarf over his shoulders. 'Stay here, K9. You're in charge.'

'Master.'

The Doctor found Romana lying on her bed in her ornate

quarters. The door was open and he paused for a moment at the threshold, regarding her solemnly. Her head moved very slightly to one side, then back again. She knew he was there.

The Doctor was astute enough to guess what was wrong. 'Do you mind if I come in?' he asked, and gave what he hoped would be an encouraging smile.

'The Time Lords want me back.'

So he was right. Not quite knowing what move to make, the Doctor entered the room, occupying himself by lifting a small, decoratively bound book from a chair as he passed, flicking through its pages as he spoke. 'Yes,' he said, 'well, you only came to help with the quest for the Key to Time.' A smile. 'I suppose they reckon you've served your sentence now.'

Romana let out a despairing sigh that chilled the Doctor. Sitting up and swinging her legs onto the floor, she explained, 'Doctor, I don't want to spend the rest of my life on Gallifrey. After all this, all the different kinds of everything outside Gallifrey, one planet becomes so tiny. I want to go on learning, Doctor. Life on Gallifrey is so static and futile.'

'You can't fight the Time Lords, Romana.' There was a grim finality in the Doctor's tone.

Romana stood and crossed to him. 'You did – once,' she reminded him.

The Doctor lifted his head from the book, staring into nowhere, allowing the bitter-sweet memories to wash over him. His days as a fugitive from the Time Lords were long behind him now. 'I lost my fight, Romana. Remember that.'

Romana ran a hand despondently through her long blonde hair. The Doctor had made his point. There could be no question of ignoring the summons.

A Time Lord summons cannot be ignored.

'Then there's nothing more to discuss, is there?' she said. 'We have to go.'

The Doctor nodded, sorry for her. 'I'm afraid so.'

K9 circled the TARDIS console, stopped, and extended his antenna towards one of the control facets. Flight data flowed into him instantly.

'Course set and holding. ETA on Gallifrey – thirty-two minutes. Flight path is clear.'

Then, an anomaly. In a gesture that was endearingly human, K9's head rose up slightly. 'Wait. Sensors indicate – no vocabulary available. Cannot comprehend. Cannot ...'

The peculiar blue London police-box shell of the trans-dimensional TARDIS suddenly exploded, an eruption of myriad slivers of blue light racing away in all directions. There was not the slightest sound, and when it was done the TARDIS remained impossibly fully intact, but distorted, continually shifting its shape, its dimensions seemingly totally out of control.

Within the craft, exactly the same was happening. The control room lengthened and shrank, its colours shifting through every spectral possibility.

K9 himself was being distorted along with the room. Though no one heard, he reported, 'I have lost control of the TARDIS.'

Wherever the TARDIS was headed in this inexplicable condition, it was beyond anyone's ability to do anything about it.

In Romana's room, the Doctor and Romana clutched desperately for some support as the room dipped and swayed and blurred before them. They saw the same insane dimensional instabilities in one another.

'Doctor ... what's happening?' Romana called.

The Doctor was looking round, wide-eyed and afraid. 'I don't know.'

Then it stopped. As abruptly as it had begun.

Normality was refreshing, and more than a little reassuring. The Doctor and Romana made sure they were both all right, then ran for the control room, the Doctor's long legs getting him there well before Romana. As he skidded to a halt by the console, K9 came whirring towards him. 'I have regained control, master,' he reported. 'The TARDIS has stabilised. Course realignments have been computed and laid in.'

'But what happened, K9?' the Doctor asked impatiently.

'Cannot explain.'

A concerned frown creased the Doctor's forehead. Behind him, Romana ran in, making straight for the console and running her learned eyes over the instrumentation.

'All right,' said the Doctor, turning again to face K9. 'Just give me the data.'

'Cannot comply.'

The Doctor and Romana exchanged a look of almost tangible unease. 'There must be some data,' countered the Doctor.

'Substantial data was received, master, yes. However, I am unable to assimilate it.'

The Doctor stroked his chin ponderously, trying to establish some kind of conclusion from all this. 'Give me a report of all damaged parts.'

It took K9 less than three seconds to conduct a systems check via his affinity programming with the TARDIS console. 'No damage, master. All component parts are functioning normally.'

'What?' The Doctor sounded almost disappointed. 'You mean to tell me that after going through all that, that the systems are still perfectly all right?'

'Not perfectly, master. The Adverb attributed was "normally".'

The Doctor assessed the information – or lack of it. Something had happened of which K9 had no programmed cognisance – something quite plainly violent, but which had left them apparently none the worse for wear. What could possibly –?

'Doctor, we're landing.'

The Doctor turned his head to see that the console's central column was slowing to a halt. 'Indeed we are,' he said with enthusiasm, moving to the console and turning the lever which operated the wall scanner.

The scanner doors, opposite the Doctor's position, slid apart to reveal a grey, arid desertscape stretching as far as the eye could see. In the far distance a mountain seemed to float, magically, on a carpet of grey heat-haze.

'The wilderness of Outer Gallifrey,' the Doctor intoned. A smile-tic played around the corners of his mouth. He looked

17

at Romana and saw her expression was one of total despair. 'Ready to go?' he asked with forced cheerfulness.

Romana released a dour sigh and leaned back against the console. 'If you say so,' she said, looking around forlornly.

'Oh, come on!' The Doctor's patience was all but at an end. If she was left to wallow in her own despair it would do her nothing but harm. 'It's not the end of the universe – we're home!'

Romana's head dipped lower. 'Sorry.'

'And don't apologise,' the Doctor barked at her. 'Just try and brighten up a bit.'

'I'll try.'

'You do that.' The Doctor pressed the door lever. The two huge entrance doors glided open with an electronic hum. Without another word, the Doctor marched out.

Romana sighed, looking around the room for what would probably be her last time, committing as much as she could to memory. So much had happened to her in this room. The smile prompted by her recollections gave way under a renewed surge of despair. She would have to get her things. She started for her quarters, but had not moved three paces when she heard the Doctor calling for her from outside.

There was something in his tone that made Romana run for the doors. Emerging from the TARDIS, she drew to an abrupt halt, mouth agape, staring in utter bewilderment at her surroundings.

The Doctor stood a short distance away from her, looking round. He turned to her with a serious expression. 'This isn't Gallifrey,' he said.

'It certainly isn't,' Romana concurred.

The TARDIS had not landed in the desertscape depicted on the scanner. It sat amid a verdant tapestry of magnificent sylvan splendour. Trees of breathtaking beauty grew majestically tall all around the two bemused time-travellers.

The Doctor was not yet aware that the TARDIS had set down on the planet Alzarius.

2

'I'm an Elite'

The three great men walked purposefully along the gleamingly immaculate starliner passageway, moving through what had once been passenger recreation areas, now study areas for the children of the community, towards Dexeter's science research area.

They were the Deciders. The three leaders of the starliner community, revered and respected by all citizens.

First Decider Exmon Draith was a staunch, hardy character, well suited to the position of having ultimate control over the lives of what were now thousands of souls. Despite this position of responsibility, however, his two colleagues, Decider Ragen Nefred and Decider Jaynis Garif, actually rated as his equals on most matters. Where a decision had to be made, democracy was the key. Any two Deciders could over-rule the third, even if that third Decider was Draith. The only instance in which Draith could overrule the unanimous votes of his two fellow-Deciders was when the System Files came into play.

No one could view the System Files except the First Decider. They held information on the history of the starliner community, going back over its many, many generations, back to and beyond the time of the crash. Information that had been deemed best kept from the people. Nobody had ever questioned this. Discipline and loyalty were the bases for the community's survival. And so the system could work. If Draith were to say that the System Files indicated one path should be followed in favour of another, that would be sufficient for his instructions to be carried through.

For the same reasons, no one questioned the classification of citizens at birth. Encephalographic scans dictated whether a person should be designated a Norm – to receive only a minimal education – or an Elite – to receive superior education in all the sciences appropriate to the survival and progression of the Community; mathematics, engineering, physics, chemistry, etc. It was established practice that only Elites could become Deciders.

Draith spared glances for the traces of welding lines which occasionally scarred the walls of the starliner. The reconstruction by their ancestors of the vessel, now being maintained by the present generation of citizens, had been a marvellous engineering achievement. And, of course, vital to their survival when the mists came ...

Draith's blood chilled at the very thought. He hoped Dexter's predictions were wrong, but he knew the man too well to hold that hope too strongly.

They arrived at Dexeter's Science Unit, drawing curious and even worried looks from citizens in the area round about. Rumours were beginning to spread, Draith knew – it was hard to keep this sort of thing quiet, and Dexeter's by now very frequent forays to the riverside harvest sites, collecting botanical specimens, had served only to fuel the speculation.

Within the Science Unit, Dexter was waiting for them, standing by a lab workbench. The room was in darkness save for a bright blue lamp over the bench. It illuminated a number of slides, several chunks of riverfruit, a high-power microscope and a scattered collection of scientific instruments, most of which looked like cutting tools of some kind.

Garif closed and secured the doors, and the three Deciders crossed over to Dexter, past a large operating couch, gathering round the cluttered bench, an ominous assembly in the stark blue light.

Draith inwardly assessed Dexter: he was in his late thirties, a frenetic, urgent character usually, but for the moment he looked unsettlingly grave.

'Well?' said Draith.

Dexter gestured to the samples of riverfruit in front of him.

20

Riverfruits grew in vast abundance in rivers all over the planet – or at least that small area of the planet they had been able to explore. They looked much like melons, and were the staple diet of the community.

'The evidence is here,' said Dexeter. 'And it's not good.'

Garif let out a despairing, patronising sigh. 'Meaning what, exactly, Dexeter?'

Dexeter lifted a half riverfruit and proffered it to them for examination. 'Look,' he said, lifting a small pair of tweezers and carefully prodding at the red-brown mush of the riverfruit's interior. The Deciders noticed a number of small, white objects imbedded among the yellow seeds.

'What are they?' Nefred inquired, voice hushed.

'They seem to be ... moving,' Draith noticed, peering more closely.

Dexeter nodded. 'It's the same sign noted in the studies of Corellis and Dell, fifty years ago. It was postulated that they might be eggs of some sort.'

Draith's eyes narrowed. 'Insect eggs.'

'Perhaps.' Dexeter's eyes scanned all three Deciders. 'Unfamiliar insect life is, by what we've previously considered to be common superstition, supposed to precede each ... incident.'

Draith turned away from the bench, looking into the shadows beyond their haven of blue light. 'Yes, that's true.'

Even his fellow-Deciders started at this.

'Can you confirm this?' asked Dexeter excitedly. 'Is it mentioned in the System Files?'

'You over-reach yourself, Dexeter,' Nefred warned.

'I cannot discuss the System Files,' said Draith, his expression pained. 'Sometimes I wish I could share it with someone, but Dexeter, I too must obey the procedure.'

Dexeter wished he could share Draith's secrets. The man knew things ... great things. He had knowledge that would surely serve a better purpose in the hands of a scientist.

Yet Dexeter was a loyal citizen, and so he suppressed these thoughts, and indicated the bench microscope. 'Take a look at this. A sample of riverfruit. I've placed the slide.'

Draith peered into the microscope eyepieces. The cell-patterns he perceived made no sense to him. He looked up at Dexter. 'What am I supposed to be seeing?'

Dexter removed the slide from the microscope and held it cautiously. 'This sample contains an embryo spider ... one which should grow to a length of between one and two feet.'

Nefred and Garif strove to find something to say, but could not.

Draith and Dexter stared levelly at each other. Draith said, quietly, 'Dexter, take me with you to one of the harvest sites. I want to look for myself. Then I'll decide whether the order should be given for everyone to be recalled to the starliner.'

Dexter was aghast. 'But Decider, on the basis of this evidence, surely you have to make an immediate –'

'I'll meet you in the boarding area in fifteen minutes.' With that, Draith turned and left.

Dexter sighed, resigning himself to the situation. 'The man's impossible,' he said. 'He's going to hang on until the last moment.'

'We all have to accommodate our acquaintances' short-comings, Dexter,' Nefred chided.

Dexter muttered something under his breath which Nefred didn't quite catch, and, as he destroyed the slide specimen with a few droplets of acid, remarked, 'You know, from a scientific perspective, I find myself almost hoping that this *is* Mistfall.'

Garif smirked, without humour. 'You're too young to remember the last one, Dexter. But it's not something I look forward to.'

'Nor I,' Nefred concurred.

As Dexter regarded the smouldering mess where once the spider embryo had been, he found himself trying to imagine what it would have looked like fully grown.

And then he tried not to imagine.

'We can't take off until we find out precisely what's happened to the TARDIS,' the Doctor had said, and had then immersed himself in the internal workings of the console. Despite the occasional bang and fountains of sparks, he had insisted that he knew what he was doing, and insisted that

Romana leave him alone. So now she sat on the grass outside the TARDIS doors, enjoying the sun on her face and the colour of the landscape.

It struck her as odd that despite the sun the air felt very cold. Dismissing this thought, she considered their situation.

The scanner had continued to show the Gallifreyan desertscape, and Gallifrey it certainly was. The co-ordinates were aligned to the precise settings. K9 reaffirmed time and again that the navigational systems were working perfectly. And yet when they stepped out of the door they were in a forest on some alien planet or other.

Contemplating the problem, Romana in time fell asleep.

And, in sleep, she was unaware of the probing tendrils of grey vapour squirming menacingly through the nearby foliage.

They were called Outlers because in the starliner community neat classifications were always desirable. Classifications made things identifiable, made them tangible and thus less frightening.

They were in actuality youngsters with few principles of behaviour other than that they had totally dissociated themselves from the way of life in the starliner community. Regarded as outcasts, they lived by their wits. The community supplied them infrequently with riverfruits. The supply was laughably small and they had to make regular raids on the riverfruit harvests to keep themselves alive.

Of course, the raids weren't always successful. Like the one this morning. They had been spied hiding by the riverfruit store and had been chased through the forest by the furious citizens. They had only just managed to escape.

Their way of life was hard – their 'home' was a cave overlooking the valley which housed the starliner. Old boxes, crates and some conveniently placed stones constituted the cave's meagre furnishings.

Adric stood in the middle of the cave floor in his fine clothes – clothes befitting an Elite – looking round at the crudeness with which the Outlers lived, wondering if he could become used to it.

Anything was better than spending the rest of his life in the predictable, sterile environment of the starliner, he told himself, unconsciously echoing Romana's sentiments towards Gallifrey.

Adric's diminutive stature and his youth belied the fact that he had one of the keenest intelligences on the starliner, an intelligence marred only by the occasional lapse into the naive mannerisms of the juvenile. Adric was an elite among Elites, outstanding in all the fields of education he had undertaken. He wore the Star of Mathematical Excellence on his tunic breast-pocket – very few of *them* had ever been awarded.

Ironically, it was Adric's brother who headed the Outlers. Varsh was slightly older than Adric, by some three and a half years, and they shared very few physical similarities, but an astute observer would have noticed a common philosophical drive in the two young men – both liked to be free of strictures, to be in charge of situations. Adric had tried to satisfy this facet of his personality by working hard to establish himself academically. Varsh had taken another route by leaving the starliner, along with two friends, Tylos Milren and Keara Login, daughter of Halrin Login, the starliner's chief engineer. Other youngsters had joined them in time. They had not been the first to leave the starliner – but they were the first ones to have done so and to have survived for so long.

Now Varsh sipped water from a crude wooden cup, grimaced at the taste, and said, 'You want to be an Outler?'

Adric clasped his brother's shoulder. 'I'm serious,' he vowed.

Tylos stood nearby, honing his knife on a small stone in his hand with ominous vigour. He was an aggressive character, his eyes wild and semi-maniacal, and it was common knowledge that he very much expected to be leader of the Outlers one day – by one method or another. 'Nobody joins us unless we all agree,' he reminded Varsh.

Varsh sipped at his drink again, and Keara came forward. She was beautiful – the problem being that she knew it. She considered Adric with a disdainful sneer and remarked, 'This one belongs in the Great Hall of Books ... with all the rest of his kind.'

'He doesn't belong here, that's for sure,' said Tylos. He approached Varsh. 'We said at the start, Varsh, we said we wouldn't accept any Elites ... unless you want to make special rules for your brother.'

Varsh's jaw stiffened angrily. He had always felt close to Adric, felt a need to protect his younger brother. Adric had been a year old when their parents had been killed in the last forest fire. They had then been brought up by friends of their parents, but had never felt they could properly express themselves to anyone except each other.

Until Varsh had decided to leave the starliner.

'We broke all family ties when we left the community,' he said, looking at Adric and hoping he knew he didn't mean it.

'Look,' said Adric, very aware of the tension between Tylos and his brother, 'I know all this. But I don't expect special treatment.'

'Don't you?' said Keara, sauntering up to him haughtily. She gestured to his tunic pocket. 'Isn't that what the star's for?'

'*That*,' said Adric, tapping it with his finger, 'is for Mathematical Excellence.'

'It's a pretty little thing,' said Keara with a smile. 'I do believe I'll take it.'

She was reaching out for it when Adric's hand clamped tightly around her wrist. He twisted, pulled, and she spun and crashed to the floor.

'I'll warn you just once,' said Adric. 'And I'm talking to all of you. Don't try to push me around. And don't ever try to tell me what to do. I've had enough of that on the starliner.'

'You'll find it worse here,' said Varsh. 'When you're struggling to stay alive the discipline is even harder.'

Adric nodded his head towards Tylos and Keara. 'Then perhaps you should keep these two in better check.'

'See!' Keara growled, nursing her smarting wrist. 'He talks like a Decider already.'

Tylos faced Adric, mustering the best threatening look in his extensive arsenal. 'If you think you'd be holding some kind of authority here, think again. You're no better than us.'

Adric seemed amused. 'Of course I'm better than you. I'm

25

an Elite.' He smirked. 'You can't even organise a raid on the riverfruits properly.' He had heard about the morning's fiasco.

Tylos scowled. 'Could you do better?'

Adric smiled his reply. 'It would be an effort to do as badly.'

Varsh was worried. He saw what was coming. 'Adric, go back to the starliner. You don't belong –'

'No,' Tylos cut in, removing a belt fashioned from marsh reeds from around his waist. All the Outlers wore them. He held it up before Adric's face. 'Know what this is?' he said. 'It's *our* badge ... and it has to be earned. Know what I mean?'

Adric stared at the belt, then at Varsh. His brother was concerned for him. But he couldn't back down now.

He said, 'It'll be easy,' with a brash confidence which he did not really possess.

The appearance of Dexeter and Decider Draith at one of the riverfruit harvests prompted subdued murmurs among the harvesters. Whatever it was that was happening, it was serious for the First Decider to be involved so directly. The harvesters noticed that the two men took a keen interest in the pile of riverfruits stacked on the bank, selecting a couple and hacking them open, then looking very worried and speaking quickly and very quietly to one another, apparently cautious of any of the harvesters who came too near.

No one noticed the Outlers taking up position by some nearby trees.

Varsh gestured everyone to silence. As they waited, watching, he secretly crossed his fingers for Adric.

There he was.

He could just be discerned slinking tentatively through a clump of bushes further along the bank, making his way towards the stack of riverfruits.

Varsh was the first to recognise the two figures by the riverfruits. 'Decider Draith's over there!' he said. 'And Dexeter, too!'

'Your brother can't see them,' said Keara. 'They're blocked from his view by the riverfruits.'

With an almost silent snigger, Tylos observed, 'Life's nothing without the occasional surprise or two.'

26

He laughed, unaware of the mists that were gradually penetrating the trees and bushes behind them, moving closer to them all the time.

Amid the foliage on the far side of the riverfruit store, Adric stopped in a position where he could see the riverfruits without being seen himself by the harvesters. The palpitations in his chest told him he wasn't as sure of himself as he would like to think. Every muscle in his body tensed. He would have to be quick. He would have to be silent. With a bit of luck –

He was about to go when he heard the screams.

They came from the direction of the river, and Adric realised there was terror in them. Just as he was about to crawl out a little further to see, Draith and Dexeter stepped out from behind the pile of riverfruits. He made a desperate sideways lunge for cover, lying with his face in the dirt and praying he hadn't been seen.

He needn't have worried. Draith and Dexeter were running towards the water, out of which the hysterical citizens were running in one screaming mass, kicking up a wall of spray. They gathered on the bank, staring at the river with horror.

It was bubbling furiously, the bubbles bursting to emit plumes of a thick grey gas which floated clumsily on the air.

Draith and Dexeter made their way to the front of the crowd. Looking on the eerie, terrifying sight, they knew their fears were soon to be realised.

Mistfall was beginning.

Draith turned to the citizens, raising his staff, and with Dexeter's help gestured them to silence. 'Calm down!' he called out. 'Calm down, all of you!'

It was not long before everyone was silent. Respect and obedience towards a Decider were cultivated in citizens from birth.

As Draith began his announcement and his warning, Adric and the Outlers listened intently from their hiding places.

'Citizens,' Draith began, his eyes scanning the frightened faces grouped around him, 'as First Decider and Keeper of the System Files, I have to announce to you the coming of Mistfall.'

Respect and obedience cultivated or not, this was a shock and it took some time for Draith to quell the frightened jabber.

'There is no need for alarm,' he assured them, 'so long as you all follow the procedure.' He paused to allow that point to sink in. 'You have two hours.' He gestured for them to be moving, and immediately they started gathering up their tools and their bags.

Draith and Dexeter moved back to the water's edge and stood contemplating the seething, gargling mass before them.

'You know,' Draith confided in a low voice, 'if the citizens knew what I know from the System Files about Mistfall ... we would never be able to maintain control over them.'

Dexeter was dumbstruck by the Decider's candour.

From where he lay, Adric could see the riverfruits lying unguarded, just a short distance away.

Mistfall. He had been instructed in the legend from birth, as they all had. The mere word itself had all the sinister connotations of the 'bogey-man' ... and Adric had not believed. It was Varsh who had convinced him, as he had convinced Tylos and Keara and the other Outlers.

It had been Varsh's theory that Mistfall was a device created by the Deciders to keep the citizens dependent upon the starliner and thus controllable – a myth. But now no longer a myth, Mistfall was happening.

And yet, despite his fear, Adric could not take his eyes off the riverfruits. The Outlers were watching, he knew. What better way to prove his bravery than by going ahead with it even after all this?

Adric found himself rising to his feet, stalking cautiously towards the riverfruits.

When Varsh saw what his younger brother was doing he was only just able to quell a shout to make him turn and run. Adric had made his decision ... he couldn't be stopped.

Draith turned from the water's edge, considering the vast responsibility which would rest on his shoulders over the coming years of siege caused by the planet's evolutionary proclivities.

Then he saw Adric.

A fierce rage coursed through Draith as he saw the boy scooping up armfuls of riverfruit, a rage at the insolence of the boy at a time like this. 'Adric!' he snarled, sending his sturdy frame lumbering towards the youngster.

Adric's head shot up at the sound of his name. Seeing Draith bearing down on him, he turned and ran, scattering the riverfruits, his mind racing, in an instant regretting ever having thought of going through with this.

Dexeter watched, perplexed, as Draith pursued the young thief.

'Decider, come back!' he cried. 'He's not worth it!'

But Draith was gone.

From their place of concealment, the Outlers had seen it all.

'Split up,' Varsh ordered. 'We'll meet back at the cave.'

They turned and started at the sight of the thick wall of mist which confronted them. It hid everything from their view.

Varsh steeled himself, shouted, 'Come on!' and ran into the mist. Tylos, Keara and the others followed, taking different routes away from the place.

Adric ran blindly through the forest, thrusting branches and shrubs to one side without once breaking his stride. There was a fear in him, a cold, stabbing fear, and that fear had a name ... shame.

Behind him, over the sound of his own rapid breathing, he could hear Draith's heavy footfalls. the old man was moving very quickly – his fitness was legendary.

Adric was unaware that all around him the mist was getting thicker.

He almost ran into a marsh, had to check himself sharply and veer to the right, running along the water's edge.

Had he the time to do so, Adric might have noticed that the mist seemed suspended particularly thickly over the waters of the marsh.

Suddenly Adric was falling. His right knee cracked off a

rock and this sent a sharp pain through his whole body. He rolled over, looking down at his knee and seeing an ugly, bloody mess through the tattered cloth of his trousers. Gazing beyond the knee, he saw the half-hidden tree root which had caught his foot. He cursed quietly.

And then Draith was there, standing over him, laying down his staff and extending a hand to the boy. 'Come on, Adric,' he said gruffly. 'They're closing the starliner.'

Adric struck out at the hand and clambered to his feet. 'Leave me alone,' he said.

'Adric, you little fool ...' Draith tried to grab him and Adric lurched to one side as the man's hand caught his shoulder. The Decider was caught off balance, and with a shout fell over, his head striking a rock, his flailing legs landing with a splash in the water. Draith lay there, eyes closed, unmoving.

Adric became worried. He moved closer to the old man, concern on his face. 'Decider?' he called quietly. 'Are you all right?'

Adric was reaching out to shake him when the body moved. Just perceptibly. Adric instinctively took a step back, suspecting a feint from the Decider.

But then he moved again, and it was clear that he was not the one responsible. Draith was moving slowly into the water. Adric gaped at the marsh. There was something in there, something under the water, which had taken hold of Draith and was dragging him in.

Adric clutched at Draith's tunic shoulders, fighting to win him back from the water.

Draith stirred, moaning, slowly regaining consciousness.

'Wake up!' Adric cried. 'Wake up!' He knew he was losing to the superior strength of whatever lay concealed beneath the surface of the marsh.

Now that Draith was almost completely under, Adric found that in his attempts to keep a hold he, too, was being dragged into the water. His feet were submerged and beginning to sink into the mud when he felt something – it felt like a hand – close around his right ankle. In his shock, he released Draith and pulled at his trapped foot, freeing himself with a jerk and staggering back to collapse on the bank.

From where he lay he saw Draith thrashing around on the surface of the water, arms flailing wildly. Fighting to keep his head above water for just long enough, he looked towards Adric and shouted a message.

'Tell Dexeter ... tell him we've come full circle, Adric! Tell him!'

Draith went down for the last time. Adric saw one hand break the surface for a moment, rising through the thin carpet of grey vapour which covered the water to clutch pathetically at the air, then it disappeared beneath the water for the last time.

The scene was ominously still. Adric rose to his feet, white with fear – then turned and ran into the mists, whimpering with claustrophobic terror as he crashed through the undergrowth.

He kept recalling the feel of that thing (that *hand*?) around his foot.

3

'Master – Alert'

The boarding area of the starliner was awash with people
thronging into the ship from the gradually more threatening
planet terrain. After identifying themselves to a tally man at
his desk near the door, they hurried off into the benign
warmth of the ship while he scribbled their names in the thick
ledger supplied for the purpose.

Amid all the relieved, frightened, and numbed faces,
Nefred and Garif, overseeing the boarding operation,
perceived Halrin Login, Keara's father. Login was a
respected man, a wise man destined perhaps one day to be a
Decider.

Login waited by the door, peering anxiously out onto the
planet's surface. The mists made visibility poor, however, so
he turned back, moving towards Nefred and Garif. 'Sirs,' he
began, 'excuse me, but ...?'

Nefred smiled sympathetically. 'Your daughter?'

'To leave her out there, with no protection,' said Login, his
consternation obvious. 'Is there nothing we can do?'

'She and the other Outlers chose to leave us, Login.'

'But Keara is so young.'

'And you, Login,' said Nefred sincerely, 'are a greatly
valued citizen. But we cannot change the law for you.'

'Nor for Decider Draith,' Garif put in. 'He too has only one
hour in which to return.'

Login frowned at the mention of the First Decider's name.
'Is he out there?'

'Yes. Because of your daughter and her friends.'

32

The two Outlers, Hektir and Yenik, charged blindly through the foliage, urging one another on.

Bursting from a particularly thick clump of bushes, they found themselves next to an expanse of watery marshland. They stopped to catch their breath.

'Let's cut across the marsh,' said Hektir.

Yenik hesitated. 'I don't know ... it might be dangerous. We don't know how deep it is.'

'Have faith, Yenik,' said Hektir with a smile. 'Come on. These thorns are cutting me to pieces. I want to get back to the cave before this mist gets any thicker.' Without waiting for an answer from Yenik, he waded quickly into the water. It went up to his waist.

'Wait for me!' Yenik cried, and lumbered after his friend. The two boys moved quickly and noisily through the water.

It was a fairly short distance to the other side.

'Hurry up, Yenik,' Hektir urged as he began to lift himself out of the murky water.

Yenik stopped suddenly, aghast, as he saw the slimy, scaly hand rising out of the water behind Hektir, reaching up for his friend's head.

'Hektir!' Yenik screamed, too late, as the hand grabbed a clump of Hektir's hair. Hektir was half-way out of the water. The hand pulled and he screamed as he fell back under the surface of the water.

It was a huge, loud splash, throwing a fountain of water into the air. Yenik stood rooted to the spot, staring at the water where Hektir had gone under until it was perfectly smooth and undisturbed.

It was as if Hektir had never existed.

Yenik was standing in the middle of the expanse of water, feeling cold and very afraid, wondering what the something was that was in the water with him, wondering when it would strike ...

For some good time he stood there, unmoving, staring fixedly at the muddy bank some eight or ten feet away from him.

Hektir's boot print. He could see it.

How fast could he move eight or ten feet across water?

He was about to try it when they struck. Not one, but three of them, leaping up out of the water around him, screaming, landing on him and dragging him under. It was over in an instant.

The water settled.

It was as if no one had ever been there.

The boarding area was almost empty. Nearly all the citizens were on board now – just one or two due in from the more remote harvest sites.

Login was still there, waiting, growing more anxious by the minute.

Nefred, standing by the door, was joined by Garif.

'Not long now,' Nefred remarked.

Quietly, as if wanting no one else to hear, Garif explained, 'When that door closes, you will be First Decider.'

Nefred's lips set in a firm, staunch line which told Garif he was well aware of the fact. 'And we shall need a third,' he pointed out.

Both men looked towards Login.

Adric drew to a halt in a small clearing on hearing the shrill, cutting whine of the Mistfall Siren. Emanating from the starliner, it was the signal that the doors were about to close. His legs sagged and he had to hold on to the trunk of a tree to prevent himself from collapsing on the ground.

He had no hope of reaching the starliner in time.

With melancholy sweeping over him like a cold tide, Adric lifted his head ... and saw the TARDIS.

It stood on the other side of the clearing, a blue incongruity. At first glance he took it for a monolith, but now, looking more closely, he saw it had doors. Not entirely sure whether what he saw was reality or a mirage, Adric moved towards it.

The doors were ajar. He pushed on those doors and stepped inside, grimacing at the sudden burst of bright white light from the interior. As his eyes grew accustomed to the glare, he took in his surroundings – or tried to. He was standing in a large white room, in the middle of which stood what looked like an instrument bank of some kind.

Then he saw the people – a man and a woman, looking at him with perplexed expressions.

The man said something, but Adric could hear nothing over the throbbing in his head which had been developing since his escape from the marsh. Reading the man's lips, however, he could make out that he was asking, 'Who are you?'

Before Adric could answer, he passed out.

Varsh stood in the middle of the cave, trembling with fright, feeling more helpless and uncertain than he had ever felt before. Hearing the sounds of movement outside, he tensed and brought his hand to the hilt of his knife.

Keara burst from the thick wall of fog which covered the cave entrance, drawing to a halt and struggling to catch her breath. As she did so, she stared across at Varsh. Her expression said everything.

'Anything could make that water bubble,' said Varsh. 'A seismic tremor. It could be anything.'

'It could be Mistfall.'

'Mistfall's a myth.'

At this, Tylos appeared in the entrance, sweating and exhausted. He nodded outside with his head. 'Refnal and Gulner don't think so. I saw them heading back to the starliner. Hektir and Yenik should have been here by now, so they've probably gone with them.'

Varsh's jaw set angrily. 'Deserters,' he sneered.

Keara paled. 'It's just us now.'

'And Adric,' Varsh reminded her.

'You can't blame them,' said Tylos. 'Not after what happened at the river. Then there's the mists. And have you noticed? It's getting colder. All those things we believed to be lies ... they're coming true.'

'Don't let the Deciders fool you, too, Tylos,' Varsh warned. 'They've taken these things and twisted them to their own advantage.'

'You'd better be right,' said Tylos, more than a hint of menace in his voice as he moved closer to Varsh. 'Or else we're dead.'

Adric lay on the bed in Romana's quarters, ashen-faced, as the Doctor applied medication to his injured knee.

Romana smiled down on him. 'Relax, Adric,' she cooed. 'Whatever it is it can't get you in here. You're safe.'

'But the others,' said Adric weakly. 'I have to warn them.'

The Doctor, in the middle of applying a bandage, raised an interested eyebrow. 'Warn them?'

'About Mistfall. My brother says it's a myth. The Outlers all think the Deciders are lying. But I've seen it.'

The Doctor, finished with Adric's wound, now leaned closer to the boy. 'Tell me about this "Mistfall",' he said.

'Decider Draith is too late.'

Garif nodded at Nefred's proclamation. Together, they turned towards the entrance. 'Seal the door,' Nefred ordered.

A citizen punched out a sequence of buttons on the panel next to the entrance. Login watched on, distraught, knowing he could do nothing. The heavy door started to descend into place.

At the last moment, two figures erupted from the fog, scrabbling underneath the door and pulling their feet in just before the panel shut out the rest of the planet.

Garif recognised them. 'Refnal and Gulner. Two of the Outlers. They were my pupils when I was a Chemistry Instructor.'

Nefred grimaced. 'What in the name of goodness has happened to them?'

Refnal and Gulner didn't lift themselves from the floor. They just lay there, whimpering.

Refnal was saying something. Nefred knelt beside him, trying to hear.

'They're ... they're coming,' Refnal whispered fearfully. 'Coming ... coming to get us.'

'We seem to be in the wrong place at the wrong time again,' the Doctor sighed, crouched on the floor of the control room as he began reassembling the console.

Romana was leaning against the wall. 'The starliner community sounds like a type D oligarchy,' she remarked.

36

'Typically, they would use propaganda like that to retain power.'

The Doctor smiled. 'Government by myth-management, eh?'

Romana winced at the atrocious pun. 'But that story about the marsh,' she said. 'He could have been hallucinating. Recreating a folk story inculcated since birth ...'

'And then again it could all be true.'

Adric appeared in the doorway. Romana gave his knee a concerned look, but her attention was taken more by his look of bewilderment as he gazed around the control room.

'That blue box I saw ...' he mused.

The Doctor climbed to his feet. 'The TARDIS, yes.'

'Is this it?'

'This is indeed, as you say, it,' said the Doctor, waving a proud hand. 'Go ahead and ask.'

'Why is it bigger inside than –?'

'Don't ask.'

As the Doctor gleefully returned to adjusting some controls on the console for calibration tests, Romana gave Adric a smile that told him she was on his side. 'We have a lot of trouble explaining that one,' she said. 'You see ...'

The Doctor suddenly whipped round, wide-eyed, and said, 'Describe the outside of the TARDIS.'

Adric frowned. 'A blue box ... it looked old, a bit scruffy. A door ... no, two doors. they opened inwards. There was a light on top I think ...'

The Doctor looked at Romana. 'This boy's not hallucinating.' He started for the doors. 'I want this place looking like a Mark IX when I get back, Romana. Come on, K9.'

Romana was taken aback by his abruptness. 'Where are you going?'

The Doctor stopped in the doorway. 'The marsh. No good sitting here theorising about it.'

'But we still don't know what's wrong with this.'

'Wrong with what?'

'The console. The scanner.' Romana sighed despairingly. 'Why can't you do one thing at a time?'

'Oh, that ... yes. Persistent image of Gallifrey.' The Doctor approached the console and from a pile of loose components he selected a small transparent box packed with intricate micro-technology. As he weighed it in his hand, he said, 'The image translator. It reads and interprets the absolute values of the co-ordinates.'

'Of course it does,' said Romana. 'Co-ordinates are only capable of having absolute values. Real space doesn't have ... negative co-ordinates.' Her face paled. The idea which had struck the Doctor seconds before now dawned on her. 'Doctor – that disruption we came through ...'

The Doctor smiled and placed the image translator down. 'It's just a thought,' he said, then turned and disappeared through the doors. K9 followed.

'It's a very nasty thought!' Romana called. 'That would mean we're out of real space altogether!'

Garif found Login sitting brooding in his quarters. The engineer lifted his head as he entered. It was customary always to greet a Decider. Login remained silent, and lowered his head again.

'Refnal and Gulner aren't saying much that's intelligible just at the moment,' said Garif, making conversation. 'But it seems they may have been pursued through the forest by a number of Marshmen. If that's so, then the rising is far earlier than it's ever been before. We only just sealed the ship in time.'

Login wasn't listening. He continued to stare at the floor, never once acknowledging the presence of the Decider.

'Your daughter is dead, Login.'

Garif saw the man's jaw tighten.

'Whether at the hands of the Marshmen or not, Login, she *is* dead,' Garif affirmed. 'The air out there cannot support life. We had to seal the doors. Don't blame us for exercising common sense.'

Login lifted his head. The anger and resentment were gone. 'If I blame anyone, it's myself,' he said quietly. 'If I'd been a proper father to her after her mother's death, she wouldn't have left me.'

'She was a disruptive element ... dangerous in an ordered society like ours, Login.'

Login asked, 'Where's our new First Decider?'

Garif paused momentarily to examine Login's tone for sarcasm or disrespect, found none, and replied, 'Nefred is receiving the System Files from bio-link storage.'

'It's hard to believe that Draith is gone.'

Garif hesitated, shuffling uncomfortably. 'Actually, there's another reason for my coming to see you . . . an immediate task for Nefred and myself will be the choosing of a new Decider.'

'Yes, of course.'

'We . . . thought of seeking your advice on the matter.'

The small room had a single light in its ceiling which illuminated a large black leather chair in the centre of the floor. Nefred sat in this chair, gave himself a moment to relax, then pressed the half-concealed button under the right arm-rest.

There was a slight hum of power as the chair sank into the floor, moving down two deck levels to the bio-link storage chamber. Nefred regarded the smooth, glistening walls of the shaft with ridiculous intensity.

Then he was in the chamber. Immediately his chair came to rest, the lights activated and Nefred saw he was seated before a data terminal.

Nefred knew that sensory devices implanted in the chair were at that very moment transferring every detail about his physical and mental make-up to the security computer which operated the terminal – a computer kept separate from all others on the starliner.

The terminal screen activated.

YOU ARE NEFRED. COMMUNITY DECIDER. PURPOSE OF VISIT?

Nefred reached out with trembling hands and punched a sequence of keys on the terminal.

ONE: REQUEST YOU REVIEW BIO-STATUS OF EXMON DRAITH.

All three Deciders had a bio-link with the computer, part of the machine's programming to monitor the well-being of the community's three most important men. As long as they lived, heart beat, respiration and other vital functions were constantly relayed into the computer.

REVIEW: THIS TERMINAL RECEIVES NO BIO-DATA RE EXMON DRAITH. EXMON DRAITH IS DEAD.

A coldness swept over Nefred. It was inevitable that this should have been the response, but this cold confirmation of his colleague's fate shocked him nonetheless. Nefred was not an unambitious man, but he fervently wished Draith were back and safe in the starliner.

Nefred forced himself to punch out another sequence on the keyboard.

TWO: STATE MY IDENTITY.

STATEMENT: YOU ARE NEFRED. FIRST COMMUNITY DECIDER.

As designated by Draith. Nefred relaxed a little and punched out a new sequence.

THREE: I REQUEST ACCESS TO ALL SYSTEM FILES.

Immediately, the screen began to fill with data. The legendary System Files released all their knowledge to Ragen Nefred. They told him secrets known only to a very few over the centuries ... and when he knew all these secrets, Ragen Nefred was a shocked man.

After the terminal screen had gone blank, he deactivated the chamber lighting and sat there in the darkness contemplating the information he now held in his head.

It was going to be an awesome burden to carry.

The Doctor knelt to examine the mess of footprints in the mud at his feet. There were the signs of a scuffle as Adric had described it. The discovery of Draith's staff, lying among some nearby reeds, was enough to confirm that Adric's story was true ... and that gave cause for very grave concern.

The Doctor looked up and around at the murky, swirling folds of mist which hung on the air like devious intent made tangible.

'What do you make of this fog, K9?'

The automaton moved up beside his master and replied, 'Initial analysis indicates non-toxic.'

'Non-toxic?' the Doctor queried. That wasn't in keeping with Adric's story. The Mistfall legend said that the mists were lethal after prolonged exposure.

The Doctor suddenly scowled, peering closely at the surface of the water in front of him. Had he seen a ripple of movement, a fleeting dark shape under the surface?

He leaned closer.

'Where are you going?'

Adric stopped in the doorway and looked back at Romana. 'To warn my brother. I have to.'

Romana knew by the look on his face there would be no talking him out of it. She fished in the pockets of her dress and pulled out a small green metal orb. 'Better take this, then. It's a homing device. It'll help you find your way back to the TARDIS.'

Adric took the object and examined it. When he pressed a button on the side, it emitted a high-pitched pulsating whine. He switched it off and thanked Romana.

'What about your knee?' Romana asked. 'Are you fit enough to walk?'

'Oh, it's healed,' he said. Noting the look of incredulity Romana directed at him, he reached down and whipped off the bandage.

Underneath, there was no sign of there ever having been an injury. The tissue had mended perfectly.

Romana was astounded.

The Doctor narrowed his eyes as he stared into the water. There was no sign of movement now. Had his eyes deceived him?

The whirring of K9's ears interrupted his thoughts.

'Master – alert.'

The Doctor looked down at his metal companion. Then, hearing the sounds of disturbed water, he looked back at the marsh.

They rose from the waters of the marshland one by one, tall, powerful, scaly creatures, dripping mud and slime. Their clawed hands tore at the air around them as sounds of inhuman ferocity were released from their throats.

They stood erect, sucking in breath, and by the nature of

their stance declared that they claimed this territory as their own.

The Doctor tensed. He had nowhere to run.

4

'We're Taking Over Your Ship'

Amazingly, the creatures did not move. They seemed oblivious to the presence of the Doctor and K9. For the moment they stood rooted to the spot, inhaling and exhaling laboriously.

The Doctor frowned. 'They've stopped moving, K9.'

'The observation is correct.'

The Doctor shifted his position experimentally. As he had expected, the eyes of the creatures didn't follow him.

'Come on, we'd better get out of sight,' the Doctor suggested.

'*Slow* movement is advised, master.'

They moved into the shrubbery, and the Doctor took up a position where he could watch events closely.

As he surveyed the terrifying figures before him, he remembered being told by Adric of the Mistfall rhyme which all citizens learned in their childhood, written by one of the first and wisest of all Deciders, a man called Pitrus.

The Doctor remembered one verse in particular:

> *When Mistfall comes*
> *The giants leave the swamp*
> *The Marshmen walk the world*
> *The forestlands they haunt.*

These were the giants.

These were the Marshmen.

'Decider Draith is dead?'

Varsh looked almost pleadingly at Adric, but his young

brother nodded confirmation of his revelation.

Tylos was standing at Varsh's shoulder. 'Well ... "leader"?' he inquired drily.

Varsh felt a lump of fear in his throat. He stood by the cave fire, staring into its flickering scarlet heart. 'All right,' he said. 'All right, maybe I was wrong.' He turned his head to Adric, his expression threatening. 'You'd better not be lying, Adric.'

'The Doctor believed me,' said Adric unworriedly.

Keara, leaning against the wall behind Adric, said, 'Hmph. This "Doctor". I wouldn't be surprised if he turned out to be some kind of hallucination himself.'

Adric, becoming increasingly annoyed by their attitude, reached into his pocket and produced the homing device given him by Romana. 'They gave me this,' he said.

Tylos took it from him, turning the small green orb over in his hand, inspecting it.

'It's a homing device for locating the TARDIS,' Adric explained.

Tylos pressed the button on the side of the orb, and smiled slightly as the bleep started up.

Keara came forward, interested. Taking up a position behind Tylos to peer at the homing device, she said, 'They've sealed the starliner. There's no refuge for us there. But this TARDIS. If it's as big as he says ...'

Varsh smiled, glad of the opportunity to reassert his authority with a firm course of action. 'Right,' he said, drawing his knife from his belt and stroking the finely honed blade with his thumb, 'let's book ourselves a seat on this mysterious ship.'

'No!' Adric came forward, grabbing Varsh's wrist and lowering his knife. 'There's no need for that. I'm sure we'll be welcomed in the TARDIS. They're kind people.'

Varsh angrily jerked his hand free of Adric's grip. 'They're repairing their ship, you say. And they know about Mistfall. Adric, use your head. As soon as they can, they'll be leaving Alzarius. This is the only way we can make them stay.'

Adric looked all three of them in the face. Setting his jaw firmly, he said, 'I won't take you there.'

Tylos raised the orb in front of Adric's face, pressed the

button and let the bleeps continue. He chuckled.

Adric lowered his head, crestfallen.

The breathing of the Marshmen, the Doctor noticed, was beginning to regularise. They flexed their scaly arms, allowed their mouths, dribbling with hungry saliva, to gape. Scaly, metallic-looking eyelids slid back over black evil eyeballs, which then scanned the surroundings.

They started climbing from the marsh, mud slithering down their tall, horrible frames, heavy clawed feet finding a secure hold in the soil by the marsh.

It occurred to the Doctor that he had seen something like this before. The behaviour of the Marshmen was similar to that of beetles coming out of pupation. They needed time to acclimatise themselves, adjusting their physiology to fit into this new, gaseous environment as opposed to the one they had experienced under the marsh.

What the Doctor found quite staggering was the amazingly short period of time these beings seemed to require to carry through this acclimatisation process.

The Doctor watched as one of the Marshmen stooped to lift a long, hefty fallen branch from the forest floor. He turned to face his fellow Marshmen, wielding the length of wood threateningly, asserting his authority.

None of the others stepped forward to challenge him.

The leader is elected unopposed, the Doctor remarked drily to himself.

With a wave of his club, the Marshman now in command conducted the others away from the marsh-side. They crashed indelicately through the shrubbery, oblivious to all obstacles. Soon they had disappeared, swallowed up in the density of the fog, until even the sounds of their progress through the foliage were doused by the fog too.

The Doctor emerged from hiding, K9 trundling along dutifully by his side. He thoughtfully regarded the spot in the white wall of fog into which the creatures had disappeared. 'Follow them, K9. Let me know where they settle.'

'Master.' The loyal computer moved off into the fog,

leaving the Doctor completely alone in the now totally silent area around the marsh.

Moisture from the mists had gathered on the Doctor's hair. Lifting one hand, he gently patted his hair with the palm, gathering some of that moisture on it. He looked at his palm, sniffed it, sampled some of the moisture with a minuscule lap of his tongue. He nodded. Definitely non-toxic. The flaw in Adric's story remained, when everything else seemed confirmed. The Doctor couldn't help but feel there was some deadly significance to this.

Behind him, the becalmed surface of the marsh broke again.

Hearing the movement, the Doctor wheeled round in an instant. His look of stark fear gave way to one of curiosity.

Standing in the marsh was a small, diminutive marsh creature. The noises it made were swinish whimpers. It cowered at the sight of the Doctor, afraid and uncertain.

The Doctor realised that it was a child.

He smiled and offered his hands paternally. 'Hello,' he said.

The Marshchild squealed and went down under the marsh again.

The Doctor was hurt.

He suddenly became aware he was alone, and in the open. Time he was getting back to the TARDIS. With one last look towards the marsh and a thought for the Marshchild, he walked off in the direction he and K9 had come.

He again studied the flavour of the moisture from his hair.

The TARDIS console was almost completely reassembled – only the image translator remained. Romana regarded it pensively, averting her eyes to her scribbled ramblings in the notepad in her hand. Negative co-ordinates, she mused. Negative co-ordinates ...

Behind her, she heard a knock on the door. Absently, she depressed the door lever and turned back to her notes.

She heard footsteps coming into the TARDIS behind her.

'Doctor,' she began, 'I've calculated that –'

The knife which appeared suddenly at her throat cut short her conversation and threatened to cut a good deal more. She saw the face of the boy wielding the weapon – a wide-eyed, gleeful face – a face with madness in it. Romana was afraid.

While Tylos held Romana steady, Varsh and Keara, knives drawn, moved round in front of her. Their faces were stern.

Varsh came in close to her. When he spoke she could smell the foul stench of untended teeth. 'We're taking over your ship,' he announced.

Romana cast her eyes past him, towards the doors, and saw Adric standing there.

With a shameful expression, he deactivated the homing orb. It fell from his fingers, hitting the floor with a clang.

He brought his foot down on it.

In the engine room of the starliner, Nefred stood precariously close to the edge of a narrow engineering throughway, gazing down on the throbbing red ion-drive cells housed in their massive protective force casings. It had been dictated that it would be many generations before the community could develop the ability to safely connect up these power cells – refurbished through solar absorption over generations – to the incredibly complicated propulsion mechanism itself.

Nefred stared at the enormous cylindrical mechanism which sat at one end of the engine room. Connected to the power cells, this mechanism which contained five crystals – the all-important catalysts in the ship's drive process – was now lying idle.

The metal panelling of the throughway under Nefred's feet reverberated with someone's approach. Looking up, he saw Garif making his way tentatively towards him, quite plainly intimidated by the altitude.

'Nefred?' he called. 'I have to talk with you. Login ...' As he approached Nefred, he could see the man's blanched complexion and weary eyes. 'Nefred? Is anything wrong?'

Nefred straightened and walked past his friend. 'Garif ... I have seen the System Files.'

'As is your right,' said Garif, following behind.

'The System Files ...' Nefred rubbed at his eyelids. 'Garif, if you could but guess –'

'Only you are entitled to those secrets,' Garif put in quickly.

'Such secrets, though, Garif ... such secrets.'

Nefred's tone worried Garif. It spoke of despair – so unlike Nefred.

They were now leaving the throughway by way of a double-sealed security passage. This took them out into a reassuringly more secure-looking passageway with two reassuring walls, a reassuring ceiling and a quite deliriously reassuring floor.

'Nefred,' Garif began, steeling himself. 'About Login ...'

'Login is very probably the most respected citizen in the community,' Nefred suggested.

'After yourself,' Garif interjected subserviently.

Nefred stopped and gave his colleague a stern scowl. 'After no one,' he affirmed. 'We need him with us, Garif.'

'And if he won't accept the post?'

'Then I shall be very afraid.'

At that moment, Login entered the passageway. The two Deciders exchanged a look, then Nefred moved to greet the man. 'Ah, Login ...'

'I was told I'd find you both in this area,' Login explained.

'Have you made up your mind, then?' Garif inquired.

Login nodded. 'I have.'

'Do you accept the post?' Nefred asked, sounding deceptively calm.

Login looked at Nefred, then Garif, then back to Nefred. 'I do.'

The Deciders hid their elation with considerable finesse. 'Excellent,' was all Nefred had to say on the matter, in the quite false tone of an official obligation prosecuted.

Garif cleared his throat. 'And ... your daughter?'

Login straightened, his hurt plain. He remembered Garif's words earlier. 'Keara ... Keara was a disruptive element.'

'What is your first concern?'

'The welfare of the community. And the work towards the Embarkation.'

Nefred seemed distracted for a moment, then he came forward and shook Login's hand. 'Well done,' he said.

Garif offered his hand and Login took it. The Decider grinned and said, 'Welcome, Decider Login.'

K9 came to an abrupt halt at a white, bubbling stream which cut directly across his path, separating him from the Marshmen, whom he could detect ahead of him, moving further into the forest.

There was no way that K9 could traverse the stream, and so he quickly calculated that he would have to negotiate a way round it, to meet up with a projection of the route taken by the marsh creatures on the other side.

K9 was aware that statistically there was a good possibility that he would fail to achieve his objective – his vocabulary did not include the phrase 'taking a long shot'.

Tylos held Romana's arm halfway up her back, his knife still at her throat. Varsh and Keara watched her haughtily. Adric stood to one side, helpless and ignored.

'Where is this "Doctor"?' Varsh growled.

Romana remained staunchly silent.

'Tylos.'

At Varsh's command, Tylos lifted Romana's arm a little higher, pressed his blade that little bit harder against the flesh of her throat.

'Tylos, watch out!' Keara screamed.

The warning was too late. Adric had moved quickly, sprinting across the floor and grabbing Tylos from behind. Romana jumped free and the two youths struggled, Tylos trying to thrust the knife backwards towards Adric's face. Adric was able to hold the blade back mere centimetres from his right cheek.

Varsh hovered indecisively nearby, torn between two loyalties.

Adric determined on his strategy. He held Tylos's wrist firmly, then twisted his hand round. Tylos yelped at the resulting friction burn, and his knife clattered to the floor.

There was a massive general dive for Tylos's knife –

Romana was the first to reach it. Whipping it up, she directed it at Tylos's throat. The youngster backed away, terrified, as Romana advanced on him.

He found his retreat obstructed by the control console. He was trapped.

Romana surprised them all by turning the weapon round hilt-first towards Tylos. 'Your knife,' she said, smiling at his bewilderment as he took it from her.

There was an uneasy, uncertain atmosphere in the control room, a silence broken when Adric spoke up. 'I'm sorry. I am. This is all my fault.'

'What do you *want*?' Romana asked.

Varsh was left to answer. 'The Mistfall legend is coming true.'

Romana paled. 'And the Doctor's out there!'

She had started to reach for the door lever when suddenly the whole room tilted to one side. The five figures were thrown across the room, slipping helplessly down the slanting floor to crash into the wall.

The room levelled out to some degree, but as they clambered upright they could still feel a certain uneasy sway underfoot.

Adric, shaken and nursing a bang on the back of the head, asked, 'How did you do that?'

Romana looked fearfully around her. 'I ... I'm not quite sure,' she said.

Then the room tilted again, this time in the other direction, and once again they were all thrown across the floor.

Despite the fog, the Doctor's sense of direction was able to guide him back to the clearing where the TARDIS had chosen to materialise. During that walk he pondered on many things. Once he had the TARDIS instrumentation at his disposal he could carry out a number of atmospheric tests. And an energy location sweep of the surrounding forest-lands should be able to detect this starliner Adric had spoken of.

Entering the clearing, the Doctor fished in his pocket for the TARDIS key. Striding forward, he looked up and found a gust of wind clearing the fog from the area in which the TARDIS had landed.

The Doctor came to an abrupt halt.

Where the TARDIS had stood there was now only a square of flattened grass. It had vanished.

5

'We Don't Know What's Out There'

The Doctor moved forward until he was on the very spot on which the TARDIS had stood. Sliding the key back into his pocket, he looked up and around, perceiving treetops dimly through the murky vapour around him.

Then he saw the shrubbery, revealed to him by another fortuitous breeze. A trail of broken branches and trodden foliage led away from the clearing. The TARDIS had been lifted and taken in that direction.

The Doctor hurried away, guided by the trail of ruin through the undergrowth.

A small, scaly hand clutched at the trunk of a nearby tree.

The Marshchild peered round the tree with black, timid eyes, watching the Doctor depart. When the mist had closed around the Time Lord, the Marshchild moved out, following the Doctor's trail.

The control room of the TARDIS continued to dip and sway, as though the vessel were being tossed around on a stormy sea.

Romana had found a handhold on the console and was hanging on for dear life. Around her, Adric and the Outlers tumbled helplessly from one end of the floor to the other, making the most of the very brief respites between the dips.

'Varsh!' Keara cried, panic-stricken. 'What's happening?'

'I don't know!' he retorted impatiently.

Romana fixed them with a determined stare. 'Something has picked up the TARDIS,' she said.

The ship tilted again, and Romana found her hands wrenched free. She screamed as she fell back against the doors, joined by the mass of flailing limbs that was Adric and the Outlers.

The Doctor had lost the trail, he was sure of it now. The TARDIS could have been taken in any direction, he speculated, as he emerged from a particularly thick clump of trees to find himself standing on the ridge of a wide valley. Below him, through the mist, he could just discern the imposing metallic bulk of the starliner.

As good a place as any to start looking for the TARDIS, the Doctor decided, and he started down the grassy slope towards the vessel at a brisk trot.

Behind him, unnoticed, the Marshchild scampered timidly from its hiding place among the trees and followed after him.

The closer the Doctor got to the starliner, the more defined became its shape. It was a most impressive vessel – much of its design appeared to be of a decorative rather than functional nature, betraying its purpose as a commercial pleasure-liner. It was not a streamlined craft – it sat on a flat base, with two enormous barrel-like protrusions angled downwards at the front of the ship and two angled downwards at the rear, for controlled directional thrust, and two even longer barrels, which projected horizontally from the rear, for forward thrust. The Doctor also noticed, between these two rear thrusters, a large, ornately fashioned spherical engine outlet. The Doctor assumed – correctly – that this outlet would have less thrust than any of the others, but that it was probably manoeuvrable to any angle and would be used for steering the ship, making it the most important outlet of all, despite being the smallest. The Doctor rather liked that notion.

In time, he found himself at the boarding ramp beneath the staggeringly large nose of the craft. Wiping his feet on a patch of grass and adjusting his scarf in a way that he hoped would make him look presentable, the Doctor then started up the ramp.

Coming to the large metal panel that was the boarding door, he gave it a firm rap and called out, 'Hello?'

He waited, tapping his feet. Nothing happened. He tried twice more, without result, then examined the hull to either side of the door. 'Hmm,' he muttered to himself, 'No doorbell. Pity, pity, pity. Ah.' His eyes fell on a small red panel of metal within the narrow alcove of the doorway, to his left. He pressed it and it popped open to reveal an array of buttons. An attempt at using them confirmed his expectation that they had been deactivated.

The Doctor dipped into his capacious pockets and produced a short, rod-like electronic device with a miniature parabolic dish at one end – his sonic screwdriver. As he set about adjusting the settings, he muttered, 'Doctor, if I didn't know any better, I would say that we are being made to feel very definitely less than welcome. Really? How shocking. I quite agree, it is shocking, Doctor.'

The Doctor lifted the sonic screwdriver, pressed it against the spread of buttons and activated it. It whined. 'I do believe I hear a doorbell,' said the Doctor, and the panel before him slid up to reveal to him the empty expanse of the boarding area. He stepped inside, invigorated by the warmth.

'Anyone at home?' the Doctor called out. 'Anyone?' He waited. 'No one. Hmm.'

His eye fell on the tally man's desk. On it sat the ledger, a few knives and harvest tools, and a couple of riverfruits. The Doctor sidled over to the desk, picked up one of the knives and examined it.

'They seem to have maintained a pretty sound grasp of metallurgy, at least,' he remarked for no one to hear. 'Very encouraging.'

For the want of something better to do, he stabbed the knife into one of the riverfruits. It went in deep and remained there. A viscous juice dribbled from the wound.

The Doctor lifted his head. He thought he heard movement from one of the two passageways that led off from the area. 'Hello?' he called again, and moved into the passageway.

The Marshchild shuffled on board, peering round with frightened awe. Its eyes lighted on the knife in the river fruit ...

Moments later, the Doctor returned from his search of the passageway, having found no one. Automatically, he reached out to pull the knife from the riverfruit – but the knife was no longer there. It had disappeared.

The Doctor surveyed the chamber apprehensively. He became aware of the strands of vapour which had drifted in through the open door and now hung on the air around him. He shrugged off his fears, feeling that the superstition of Adric's people was beginning to affect him.

The Doctor moved over to the door, located the button display on this side of the entrance, activated it, and watched the panel slide down into place.

Still looking around, he moved along the second passageway into the starliner.

As he passed one corridor junction, the Marshchild shambled out behind him, watching him.

It set off after the Doctor.

The TARDIS was stable.

Romana, Adric and the Outlers lifted themselves off the floor with some relief, counting their injuries, which fortunately were no more than superficial.

Tylos parted from the others. 'Let's get out of here,' he urged.

Varsh shook his head. 'We don't know what's out there.'

Tylos stood before the TARDIS doors, wondering what kind of horror could lie beyond them ... his imagination began conjuring up all kinds of nasty possibilities, and to quell these thoughts he spun round and protested, 'Well, I don't trust *her*!' He indicated Romana.

Romana smiled in a way that irritated Tylos no end. 'Where do you think you'd go?' she asked. 'If this story about the mists is true?'

Tylos stammered, 'I don't know ...'

Romana dismissed him, turning to Adric. 'Is there any machinery on your planet that could lift the TARDIS?'

'How heavy is it?' Adric asked.

'In your gravity, I should imagine roughly five times ten to the six kilos.'

Adric almost laughed. 'No, nothing like that,' he answered.

'Deciders talk!' Tylos sneered.

Keara heard none of this. Her mind was on something else – the Mistfall rhyme. She had been taught by Varsh to dismiss it as propaganda, but now she recalled it within her head, word for word. She had never really forgotten it, could never forget it.

Two lines were particularly vivid. She remembered fearing that part of the rhyme more than any other as a child. To the other occupants of the room, she spoke them aloud:

'When Mistfall comes
    The giants leave the swamp ...'

There was a hush, then Varish spoke up, continuing the verse.

'The Marshmen walk the world
    The forestlands they haunt.'

Romana remembered Adric's recital of the poem.

'You're trying to scare us,' said Tylos, sounding scared. 'Are you suggesting the Marshmen carried this thing?'

'Well, let's have a look,' said Romana, and she turned the scanner control on the console. The scanner doors parted – to display a different view of the same Gallifreyan panorama.

'That's not Alzarius,' said Varsh, perplexed.

'Damn,' Romana groaned. 'It's still Gallifrey.' She closed the scanner doors and looked at Adric. 'If the Doctor's theory is right, we'll need a local image translator to see what's out there.'

'Or,' Adric proposed, 'we could always just look out through the doors.'

They all turned to look at the doors. There was no way of knowing what lay beyond them.

'There's no other way,' said Adric.

Romana had to concur. She depressed the door lever and the two large doors swung open.

Adric peered into the spatio-temporal void, pitch black, which lay between the TARDIS's inner and outer doors. 'I'll go first,' he said, and walked out through the doors.

He found the external doors a few feet into the blackness, grabbed them and pulled, and emerged ... onto the rock floor

56

of the cave which he and the other Outlers had left not three hours ago in search of the TARDIS.

There was no doubting it was the same cave – their various pieces of bric-à-brac lay scattered around, and the fire still smouldered in the centre of the floor.

The others crowded out of the TARDIS behind him.

'Curious, isn't it?' said Adric.

Keara saw them first. She screamed and pointed to the entrance.

The others looked.

The cave entrance was packed with Marshmen.

The creatures regarded the humans with glowering enmity, their thick eyelids moving slowly over their black eyes in a way that was malevolence incarnate.

The leader moved forward, club raised, and his Marshmen followed behind him. They moved slowly, apparently finding it difficult to move in this new environment. It was very probably this which saved Romana and the youngsters. They lunged as one body into the TARDIS, slamming the doors shut just as the Marshleader's club came swinging down towards them.

On the other side of the doors, Adric and Romana leaned against them, out of breath.

'Beats a boring old scanner any day of the week, eh?' said Adric.

Romana shot him a look that spoke much more eloquently than words.

The Doctor had changed his strategy.

There were things about the starliner that somehow didn't 'smell' right to him, and he had made the decision that instead of trying to contact the inhabitants of the ship right away, it might in the meantime be best if he remained at liberty to explore the vessel as he pleased, to find out for himself as much as he could about it.

What nagged at the Doctor was that the starliner seemed in too perfect a condition. He hadn't been able to find one thing wrong with it, structurally or technically. The occasional welding scar was proof enough that the ship had once been in a state of great disrepair, but the Doctor's suspicions were aroused.

He wanted a look at the ship's engines.

At the end of the passageway ahead of him he saw three citizens standing talking amongst themselves. Immediately, he ducked into an ancillary passageway and waited, pressed against the wall.

A voice from a speaker set in the wall above his head made him start. It was calling for a maintenance crew to attend a passageway junction on the fourth deck. Immediately, the three citizens he had seen moved off. The Doctor thanked his luck and moved into the now empty corridor.

At the end of the passageway he stopped, sensing movement behind him. He started to turn, hearing another shuffle of movement, but when he looked back along the passageway whatever had been there was gone.

Deciding to investigate, he moved back up the passageway and peered round the corner into the ancillary passage where he himself had hidden.

No one.

The Doctor was about to turn away with the belief that his imagination was getting the better of him when a glint of light from the floor caught his eye. Looking down, he caught his breath suddenly.

He stooped to pick up the object.

It was the knife he had stabbed into the riverfruit.

Then he heard the voices – not imagination this time – excited, agitated human voices. The Doctor pocketed the knife and hurried in the direction of the sounds.

Turning a corner, he came across a sight that sickened him.

A group of citizens, a maintenance crew, surrounded the whimpering Marshchild, threatening it with their work tools. The poor creature was pressed up against the wall, shielding its face with short, scrawny arms that waved pathetically.

The leader of the maintenance crew, a brash young man called Omril, said, 'It's a marsh creature, all right. And it's only a baby one. Can't harm us. But maybe *we* can harm *it*, eh?'

The Doctor was reminded of the time he had witnessed the

murder of a 'witch' in England on seventeenth-century Earth – a young girl, innocent, unaware of the atrocities people could perpetrate under the influence of an inbred fear. He had been too late on that occasion. Now he threw himself forward, knocking a couple of the citizens aside to get himself between them and the Marshchild. 'What do you think you're doing?' he snarled at them. 'There's no need to treat it like that – can't you see it's terrified?'

'What do you mean? It's an animal, not a person,' Omril began. Then he stopped, scowling. 'Wait – who are you?'

'A visitor,' the Doctor replied mysteriously.

'You unsealed the entrance!'

The Doctor could see now that they were the ones who were terrified. 'It's all right,' he assured them. 'I sealed it up again. Don't let appearances fool you. I'm really most awfully tidy when it comes to spaceships and the like.'

Omril regarded the Doctor levelly. 'I think the Deciders will want to talk to you.'

'The Deciders, eh?' said the Doctor. 'My, my. How thrilling!' His tone suggested it was very much less than thrilling, but, truth be told, he was rather pleased. This was a chance to get to the root of things.

'Come on,' said Omril.

The Doctor and the Marshchild were shepherded along the passageway.

'Don't worry,' the Doctor assured the small creature at his side, 'You're quite safe with me.'

They turned the corner.

'I hope.'

It is usually a very effective psychological ploy to leave someone you wish to feel inferior standing in total darkness for a period of time. It instils in most people a sense of vulnerability and paranoia.

'If you'd listened to that final reminder,' the Doctor pointed out, 'and paid the bill, this never would have happened.'

The Doctor was not 'most people'. He had been left in darkness for over half and hour.

'If you don't speak to me soon, I shall go into a huff.'

There was serious reasoning behind the Doctor's levity. He didn't speak merely to intimidate his unseen audience: the resonance of his voice enabled him to approximate the dimensions of the room in which he stood. It was large – very large. Always know your territory, the Doctor considered.

'Where is the Marshchild?' the Doctor demanded. He had played their game long enough.

'The creature is with Dexeter.'

The voice came from nowhere – the Doctor estimated that 'nowhere' was about forty feet in front of him and twenty feet above him.

'Who's Dexeter when he's at home?'

'He is the community Perceptor – expert in science, mathematics, medicine, all the necessary fields.' A pause. 'He's waited a long time for one of those things. It seems proper to let him have his fun.'

'If that child is harmed …'

'Don't threaten us, Doctor.'

'The creature will not be harmed,' came another voice. 'We are not barbarians.'

A spotlight came on and lit up the Doctor. He shoved his hands deeper into his pockets and bubbled his lips. 'Ho hum. Yes, very good. Very striking. Very visual. Very boring.'

Three more spotlights activated, one by one, illuminating Nefred, Garif and Login in turn. Over their official clothing they wore the ceremonial golden epaulettes of the Deciders in Session.

In turn, they rose to their feet and announced themselves.

All the lights went up, and the Doctor saw before him tiers of transparent cabinets packed full with books and manuals of every size and description. At the far end of the room, the Deciders sat in their galleries, Nefred, by virtue of being First Decider, occupying a level above Garif and Login.

The Doctor remembered that Adric had spoken of the Great Book Room. This was it. Despite himself, he was impressed.

'Doctor,' Nefred began, 'we are the Deciders, and we have questions to put to you.'

In the Outlers' cave, the Marshmen were gathered *en masse*

around the TARDIS, hammering it with wood, rocks, or simply their fists. There was a bestial ferocity in their actions, and yet a certain degree of co-ordination, their blows timed to inflict the optimum force on the TARDIS doors.

The Marshleader was the first to hear the sound – a low electronic hum matched with a peculiar whirring sound, coming from beyond the mouth of the cave.

The other Marshmen heard it too, and stopped their assault on the TARDIS.

Within the TARDIS, Romana had been leaning against the console, head bowed, listening to their hammering. The sudden silence made her look up, startled. She inspected the young faces around her as if expecting to find an answer in one of them. They were of course just as perplexed as she.

'Changing their tack?' Adric suggested.

Romana peered at the doors, lips pursed. 'I don't know.'

Adric steeled himself and made for the doors. 'Let's take a look.'

'No, Adric,' Varsh protested, but Romana had activated the door control. As they swung open, however, she eased herself in front of Adric. 'Stay behind me, Adric,' she warned.

Stepping into the void, Romana found the blue doors and opened them very slowly. Adric at her shoulder, she peered through into the cave, and what she saw made her brow furrow with concern.

K9 was trundling into the cave while the Marshmen regarded him with what Romana could only interpret as total astonishment. Romana tensed as she noticed the Marshleader weighing his club in his hand.

'Do not be afraid,' K9 soothed. 'I am non-hostile, operating in data acquisition mode. Explain your –'

The leader let out a shrill, horrible shriek and swung his club in an arc that brought it down on the back of K9's electronic neck. There was a brief chatter of angry sparks as K9's head was ripped from his body. It tumbled across the floor, coming to rest in a corner, while his body sat motionless, acrid fumes rising from the yawning aperture at his neck, bared wires occasionally daring to spark.

Romana felt a chill run through her. 'K9 ...' she gasped.

6

'You Will Answer the Questions, Doctor'

'That was your computer,' said Adric as he and Romana returned to the control room. She closed the doors.

'Still is, I hope,' she said. 'If the damage isn't beyond repair.'

Varsh glowered towards the doors, in his imagination seeing beyond them, into the cave. 'Senseless creatures!' he snarled.

'I don't think so,' said Romana softly. 'Have you noticed how fast they're adapting? And not just physiologically. They've obviously organised some kind of leadership. They've taken up shelter, a base of operations if you like. And their attempts to open the TARDIS doors were very systematic. That's intelligent behaviour.'

'Intelligent?' Tylos sneered. 'Trying to kill us?'

'Perhaps they have a grudge against you? This is *their* planet, after all. You're just intruders, imposing yourselves on their rightful territory.'

Keara was pondering something Romana had brought up. 'Wait a minute,' she said. 'Why do you suppose they chose this cave? There are dozens of others.'

'It does seem a little more than coincidence,' Varsh agreed.

'Why did you choose this cave?' Romana asked.

'To keep an eye on the starliner, of course,' Varsh answered.

'Yes,' said Keara. 'It looks straight down into the valley.'

'Then it would appear,' said Romana, 'that they also have an interest in the starliner. They'd like to get inside the starliner, to get at your people inside. They have intelligence ... They probably also have a plan.'

'Decider Draith? You witnessed his death?' Nefred's shrill voice carried easily across the length of the Great Book Room to the Doctor. The Doctor detected in his tone something verging on ... fear – the fear of discovery. But discovery of what? The Doctor was intrigued.

'You don't seem to be hearing me very well from up there,' he said. 'Have I got to repeat everything? Look, I'm sure all this ceremonial is considered very impressive by the general public, but it's beginning to get on my nerves. Can't we go somewhere more intimate? Some little football pitch, perhaps?'

The Deciders had no conception of what a football pitch was, and did not appreciate the humour. The Doctor could see he was going to have his work cut out for him.

'You will answer the questions, Doctor,' Garif intoned threateningly.

The Doctor's eyebrows went up.

'Decider Draith,' Login reminded him with a trace of irritation.

'Oh, that. Yes. Well, Decider Draith was dragged into the marsh. What have they got against you, these Marshmen?'

'We're investigating that question,' Garif replied.

'They seem to resent our presence as aliens,' Nefred put in.

The Doctor sighed. The same old problem. 'Why can't people be nice to one another for a change?' he said aloud. 'I mean, I'm an alien and you don't want to drag me into a marsh, do you?' He cast his gaze across their stern faces. 'Then again ...'

'How do you know this about Decider Draith,' Garif inquired, 'if you did not witness the event?'

'I had a very reliable eyewitness,' came the Doctor's reply. 'Then, when I visited the scene of the crime –'

Login interrupted him. 'You went to the marsh?' There was incredulity in his voice.

'Yes.'

'But the mists?' Login's eyes veered towards his fellow-

Deciders. 'How could you breathe?'

'There was an odd smell, certainly,' the Doctor stated. 'But definitely non-toxic.'

Login appeared shaken. 'Clearly the witness is lying. The manuals say the mists are fatal.'

Garif and Nefred looked at each other, then at Login. 'Not necessarily,' said Garif.

'Not *necessarily*?' Login stammered.

'Login,' Nefred began, 'as First Decider, I am now Keeper of the System Files.'

'The truth is known to Nefred,' Garif simpered. 'We must simply accept the inconsistency.'

'It is fitting the citizens believe the mists are dangerous,' said Nefred.

'It keeps them from straying when Mistfall comes,' Garif pointed out.

'But –'

'It is for the *good* of the community,' Nefred affirmed solidly.

Login came back angrily. 'My daughter may still be alive!'

Before the argument could continue, the doors hummed open. From beyond, Dexeter strode in. He spared the Doctor a cursory glance, then lifted his head to address the Deciders in their galleries.

'Deciders. I have examined the marsh creature.'

'And?' Nefred inquired.

'Nothing.' Dexeter sounded totally demoralised. 'No aggression. None of the characteristic traits. It's not nearly developed enough. The specimen is useless.'

'That depends on your point of view.'

Dexeter turned to the curiously garbed stranger at his left shoulder who had just spoken. He was not in the habit of being told his job by anyone. 'I'm speaking scientifically,' he explained.

The Doctor grinned and spread his hands. 'So am I.'

A shadow of a smile appeared on Dexeter's sallow face. 'You're a scientist?'

'Nice to meet you,' said the Doctor, taking Dexeter's hand and shaking it warmly. As if struck by a sudden notion, he put an arm around Dexeter's shoulder and drew him aside confidentially. 'Useless, you say? Would you care for a second opinion?'

Romana, Adric and the Outlers were taken by surprise when the TARDIS again pitched to one side. They were thrown across the room as they had been before.

'The Marshmen are lifting the TARDIS again!' Tylos cried. 'What are they doing?'

It was to Adric that the situation first revealed itself. 'The starliner! Romana!' he called.

Romana didn't understand at first. Then it struck her. 'Of course!' she said. If she was the type of person to slap her brow she would have done so. 'The momentum!'

'If the TARDIS is as heavy as you say ...'

'What is it?' Varsh wanted to know. 'What momentum?'

Romana attempted the calculations in her head. 'Accelerating down the slope – how far, Adric?'

'Say five thousand metres.'

'What are you *talking* about?' Tylos screamed, clutching at the wall as the floor swayed under him.

Romana threw herself at the console, grabbing hold and reaching out for the controls she would need. 'I think we're about to be used as a battering ram,' she explained. 'A battering ram to smash in the starliner.'

The Outlers gaped at one another.

'What can we do?' said Keara.

'Nothing. Just stand by. I'm taking off. I'll just set the co-ordinates ... five thousand metres due west.'

'You can't take off from inside a cave ... can you?' said Adric.

'I'd explain,' Romana replied with a smile. 'But I don't think even your maths is good enough. Right. Here we go.'

She was reaching for the dematerialisation switch with one slender hand when suddenly the whole room jarred with such force they were all thrown off balance and collapsed on the floor. The floor felt solid again, unmoving, settled.

They looked at one another, totally bewildered.

'What's happening now?' Adric wanted to know.

'I trust you haven't harmed it?' The threat in the Doctor's voice was none too veiled as he looked down on the body of the Marshchild, laid out on the operating couch in Dexeter's Science Unit, covered with a surgical sheet.

'Merely a little anaesthetic,' Dexeter assured the Time Lord. 'Completely humane, I assure you.'

'At least it won't cause any trouble in that condition, eh?' the Doctor growled.

Dexeter's mouth twisted wryly. 'Unfortunately.'

The Doctor scowled. 'What?'

Dexeter passed his eyes over the Marshchild and, slowly shaking his head, explained, 'It's far too passive for my purposes. I'm trying to research the psycho-dynamics of these creatures. Their motivation to attack us is immensely powerful, you know – it's well documented. But no one has yet troubled to discover why.'

'This one will have the same basic brain type, though,' said the Doctor. 'The main difference is physiological.'

Dexeter regarded the Doctor with a respect that was growing stronger all the while. 'You think so?' he asked.

'Certainly. The behavioural clues are all there. You'll just have to look a little deeper for –' The Doctor stopped himself, frowning towards the Marshchild's right arm. Lifting the sheet which half-covered it, he saw a small, rectangular patch of red where skin had once been. 'This isn't psycho-dynamics,' he growled. 'You've been taking tissue samples.'

'I try to be thorough, Doctor. It is the scientist's first prerequisite.'

'You said you wouldn't harm it.'

Dexeter responded apologetically. 'A scientist is responsible to the community, Doctor. Each of us has his task to perform.'

'Yes,' said the Doctor, beginning to move around the room, studying the apparatus, gathering information as was in his character. 'That's one thing I don't understand and I'd like you to explain to me, Dexeter. Your tasks.'

Dexeter was adjusting the sheet over the Marshchild to again conceal the ugly patch of red on its arm. 'How do you mean?'

'You're all so busy.' The Doctor waved an arm eloquently. 'Maintenance crews everywhere. What are you all up to?'

'Preparing for the Embarkation, of course.' Dexeter made it sound as if it had been a silly question.

'You're leaving Alzarius?'

'All our endeavours are directed to the return to Teradon.'

Quote-unquote, the Doctor remarked inwardly. 'If you're leaving the planet,' he asked, 'why all the fuss about the Marshmen?'

Dexeter smirked. 'The Deciders', he said, in a tone and with a short wave of the hand that dismissed them as simpletons, 'are returning us to our historic roots and our old knowledge. But my quest, Doctor, takes us forward – to knew knowledge.'

'It does? Oh, goody.'

Dexeter, with some effort, ignored the Doctor's quip and went on, 'There are anomalies unaccounted for by the Deciders. Look at this tissue sample.' At this he caught hold of the Doctor's sleeve and virtually dragged him across to the bench microscope.

At Dexeter's eager invitation, the Doctor stooped to place his eyes to the microscope eyepieces.

'Remarkable, isn't it, Doctor?' Dexeter's voice was hushed with excitement. 'The organisation of the cell structure.'

The Doctor could not become so excited. The specimen looked quite normal – a few peculiarities, as could be found in any specimen taken from an alien form of life, but nothing particularly outstanding. With a non-committal look he lifted his head from the microscope. 'That's life, Dexeter,' he placated. 'Very remarkable, I agree. But don't you think you should be getting the creature back to its natural habitat?'

'It's too late for that, Doctor.'

'In fact I'd quite like to get back to my own natural habitat, come to that,' said the Doctor. 'Tell me, old chap, you don't happen to have come across a sort of a big blue thing with a light on top, have you? It must be out there somewhere.'

'It is impossible to leave the starliner, Doctor.' Dexeter's tone was quite final. 'The doors are sealed.'

The Doctor grinned knowingly. 'Oh, I think we could

possibly arrange something.'

A deep, familiar voice came from the direction of the doors. 'What did you have in mind, Doctor?'

The Doctor whipped his head round to see Login standing in the entrance. He laughed and gave a little shrug. 'Just a hypothetical idea, Decider ... Login, is it?'

'Your entry was more than a hypothesis,' said Login. 'Perhaps our security system is not all the manuals claim?'

'Oh, you can't always go by the manuals.'

'But we do, Doctor. Without the store of knowledge in the Great Book Room we would not have survived.' He gestured towards the door. 'Doctor, I'd like you to show me how you gained access.'

The TARDIS doors opened.

Romana was the first to emerge, looking around tentatively. There wasn't a Marshman in sight. The cave seemed empty. Behind her, Adric and the Outlers craned their necks for a view, and stepped out onto the cave floor with the utmost caution.

'I wonder what –?' Varsh began. And then he saw it. The others looked at him, then followed his gaze to the stack of riverfruits in the corner.

One of the riverfruits had split open and a wet, spindly spider was emerging, forelegs quivering agitatedly in the air, its multi-faceted eyes emitting a strange, ethereal glow.

It was about a foot in length.

Romana, feeling her throat dry, said, 'So that's what frightened the Marshmen off.'

Other riverfruits were beginning to open. One at floor level split with an audible crack. A peculiar green fluid oozed out from it, spilling across the cave floor. From the mushy, glutinous material within the fruit a spider emerged, fighting its way out.

'There's more of them – look!' Tylos screamed.

As he pointed, the others turned their gaze to a dark, shadowed recess of the cave. Five or six of the spiders were emerging into the light, drawn by the sounds of the humans' presence. They stopped, gathering themselves, on the edge of the darkness, shuffling in a way that implied intelligence and was infinitely terrifying.

Romana remained where she was, looking at the spiders with curiosity. Behind her, the Outlers were bundling back inside the TARDIS. Varsh caught hold of Adric's tunic and dragged him with them.

Inside the control room, Tylos went straight to the control console, his hands wavering as he tried to remember how Romana had worked it. He pulled a switch.

Romana was jolted from her study of the spiders by the sound of the TARDIS doors slamming closed behind her. 'Adric!' she cried.

In the control room, Adric, furious, clutched Tylos's arm and threw him with strength born of anger away from the controls, sending him crashing into the wall. 'Romana's out there, you idiot!' he protested. He surveyed the bewildering array of instruments before him. 'Which one is the door control?'

Tylos was nursing a bruised shoulder. 'You're so clever, an Elite ... guess,' he sneered.

Adric didn't have the time to argue it out with Tylos. He reached forward and activated a switch. The console's central column began rising and falling. He had operated the dematerialisation switch.

Romana was hammering frantically on the TARDIS doors. She heard the engines starting up. As the TARDIS faded away before her eyes, she found her fists suddenly flailing through thin air. The TARDIS was gone.

She was alone with the spiders.

The small, black, malevolent creatures had moved around the cave wall, blocking off her route to the cave mouth, and now they came forward, moving inexorably towards her.

Romana did her best to subdue the terror that was welling up inside her. Looking around her, she searched for a weapon to use against the creatures. She grabbed the nearest object to hand – one of the riverfruits.

She was about to throw it towards the spiders when she heard a loud, snapping crack and the riverfruit split open in her hands, spilling green fluid.

The arachnoid within ejected itself from the slithering, repulsive mess, aware of the human presence.

Romana felt its eight legs gripping her face, felt its mossy-soft body pressed against her cheek, felt the bite, before her hand could swipe the repellent creature away.

Looking at the approaching spiders, she saw they had shifted out of focus. The cave was spinning around her, she could feel a peculiar hotness washing through her.

The ground came up to meet her, and then she was unconscious.

The spiders scuttled relentlessly towards her, clambering onto her body, until they covered her entirely, an undulating mass of black animosity.

7

'A Little Patience Goes a Long Way'

Adric, Varsh, Tylos and Keara stood around the control
console of the TARDIS, staring in awe at the time column as
it rose and fell, bright lights winking within it.

'What's happening?' Tylos whispered.

'I don't know,' Adric replied. After a moment's consideration, he ventured, 'We seem to be travelling.'

Keara grabbed Varsh's arm protectively and buried her
head in his shoulder. 'Varsh ... do something,' she pleaded.
'I'm frightened.'

'Adric?' Varsh called to his brother. 'You're the clever one.
Where are we going?'

'How should I know?' Adric snapped, as afraid as any of
them. 'Romana set the co-ordinates. We could be going
anywhere.'

'Anywhere ...' Keara repeated to herself.

K9's body remained where the Marshmen had left it, in the
centre of the cave floor. From his dark interior, a spider
appeared, crawling out through the opening at his neck,
pausing to assess its environment. It dropped to the floor,
landing squarely on its eight legs, and started to cross to
where the other spiders enveloped the body of Romana. On
the way, it passed the remains of the spider that had bitten
her. It lay on its back, dead, unmoving, beginning to decay.

It had served its purpose.

Login and the Doctor walked the corridors of the starliner at a brisk pace initiated by Login. The Doctor had noted that the man seemed somehow nervous, preoccupied with some inner worry. He knew the best thing to do was to leave the matter for Login to raise himself, if he wanted to raise it.

'Don't feel too badly,' said the Doctor, to start some kind of a conversation. 'There aren't many door mechanisms that can resist a sonic screwdriver ... in expert hands.'

Login gave a snort. 'Any method of breaching the starliner is of grave concern.'

'Isn't that a bit paranoid?' the Doctor considered.

'Cautious, Doctor.'

A moment later, Login found himself suddenly alone. Looking back along the passageway, he saw the Doctor had stopped next to a wall power-point where a maintenance crew were carrying out an equipment installation. From one of the citizens the Doctor had taken the piece of equipment that had just been removed and was looking at it closely. With a look of disappointment, he returned it and then caught up with Login. 'Sorry. Thought it might have been an image translator. I need one for my ship, you see.'

'Ah,' was Login's only comment as they walked on.

'Tell me, Login,' the Doctor went on, 'why are your maintenance men replacing a perfectly good optronic relay?'

Login gave the Doctor a look that showed he was genuinely bewildered, but he shrugged the matter off. 'I was installed as a Decider only recently, Doctor. I know little of these matters myself, for the time being. But I know the manuals are thorough in their requirements.'

'At this rate it could be years before the preparations are complete.'

Login laughed. 'Generations, Doctor. We have no illusions about that.'

'Generations?' The Doctor was amazed.

'There is always something to be perfected.' And again he spoke in that way the Doctor had found characteristic of all starliner citizens, as if reciting a memorised phrase. 'A little patience goes a long way.'

'And a lot of patience,' the Doctor observed, ' can go absolutely nowhere.'

72

They walked on, through a number of passageways, remaining silent, until the Doctor found that they were approaching the boarding area. Login stopped him before they entered, leaned towards him in a conspiratorial manner. 'Doctor ... you spoke of some vehicle you travel in,' he whispered.

'The TARDIS. Yes, I'm feeling rather lost without it.'

'I can help you find it,' Login offered.

The Doctor looked at the man with curiosity. 'You? Why?'

'I have a daughter,' Login answered. 'A daughter I love very much. She's out there on the surface. Possibly dead, but just as possibly alive. Help me find her, Doctor, and I'll help you find your ship.'

The Doctor considered this for a moment, then nodded. Login grinned and gave him a brief pat on the back. The two men moved into the boarding area.

The Doctor's jaw tightened as he saw that not only had there been citizens posted to make sure the starliner doors remained secure this time, but they were headed by Omril, the young man who had been so sadistically eager to taunt the Marshchild.

Omril and the Doctor looked into each other's eyes for the briefest of moments, and in that time knew all of their loathing for one another.

Login walked up to the massive boarding door. 'Unseal the entrance,' he commanded.

Omril was obviously shocked by the Decider's order. 'But, Decider ...' he stammered.

'The decision is made, Omril.'

'But I thought the decision was to keep the door sealed?'

Login moved towards the young man until their faces were mere inches apart. 'Decisions,' he said authoritatively, 'can be changed.'

Omril remained undecided, and would not have known what to do had not a further distraction appeared, in the form of a wheezing, groaning sound that entirely filled the air around them.

The citizens were beginning to panic when they saw the strange blue box gradually fading into existence in one corner of the chamber. As the object solidified, the wailing groan died away. A fearful hush fell over them all.

Login failed miserably in his attempts to retain his composure. He looked to the Doctor for some kind of answer. 'What is it?'

A wide smile stretched the Doctor's face. 'Well done, Romana,' he said quietly, then tapped on the TARDIS door. 'Romana?'

The door opened. But the head that appeared was not Romana's. The Doctor regarded the short, beautiful blonde girl with nothing short of total astonishment. 'Who are you?' he wanted to know.

The girl's eyes, worried at first, widened with delight. 'Father!'

The Doctor was taken aback. 'Oh, no,' he said. 'Hardly.'

Keara ran forward, past the Doctor, into the open arms of Login, her father. The Doctor saw the proud man's eyes were moist.

'Keara,' he said, his voice choked with emotion. 'You're safe!'

The Doctor smiled happily at the reunion, but then his attention was taken by the emergence of another figure from the TARDIS. He did not know the young man, nor the one who followed him. 'What?' the Doctor stammered, looking Varsh and Tylos up and down. 'Who are you? How do you do. Just a moment, what is this? Noah's Ark?' And then, at last, a familiar face. 'Adric! Where's Romana?'

Adric looked totally lost, confused at finding himself in this environment. 'She's not here,' he said.

'Adric, young fellow, you have a remarkable gift – an ability to grasp the patently obvious,' the Doctor chided. 'Where is she?'

'Back at the cave.'

'What cave?' The Doctor didn't wait for an answer, merely pushed past Adric and into the TARDIS. His arm emerged again, grabbed Adric and pulled him in. 'Tell me on the way,' the Doctor's voice said, and then the door slammed closed.

Login released Keara from his embrace and held her at arm's length, a single tear running from one eye as he looked upon her. 'Keara ... I never expected to see you alive. Don't ever leave me again. Promise.'

'I promise,' Keara vowed. 'I'll always be with you. Always.'

'There will have to be an inquiry,' said Login, and he noted the concern on her face and on the faces of Varsh and Tylos. 'But don't worry. I'll do all I can for you. And at least you're alive.'

He embraced Keara again, and was so filled with euphoria he was hardly aware of the sound of the TARDIS engines starting up and did not lift his head as the craft faded away in front of them all.

In the TARDIS, the Doctor manipulated a plethora of complicated mechanisms on the facets of the central console with a practised dexterity, while Adric watched on, his face drawn and guilt-ridden.

'Very odd, you know,' the Doctor remarked. 'These short hops don't usually work. And to be quite frank the chances of reversing a short trip are even more remote.' He saw that Adric, troubled, was barely listening, and decided to essay a joke. 'Still, here's hopping, eh?'

Adric didn't even smile.

The TARDIS materialised in the cave with an uncharacteristic ease which the Doctor found somehow unsettling. Deciding to ponder on it later, he led Adric out into the cave.

The Doctor paused outside the TARDIS doors, allowing his eyes to accustom themselves to the poor light. The fire in the centre of the floor was by now no more than an untidy heap of ashes.

'There she is, Doctor.'

The Doctor followed Adric's pointing finger, and could just discern a vague form among the shadows in one of the cave's deeper recesses. He moved into the shadows, Adric behind him, and found himself standing before Romana. She sat on a rock, unworried, staring straight ahead. It was as though she was unaware of their presence.

The Doctor was about to speak when something moved at

his feet, a small, scuttling shape. Adric darted forward and kicked at it. The spider careered away across the cave floor, its stick-like legs flailing urgently.

The Doctor and Adric remained totally silent and still as from the black corners of the cave they heard a chorus of hurried clickings.

'Doctor ...' Adric could barely contain his fear as the spiders ventured forwards into the light. They were a solid line, all around, exercising the same strategy as they had used on Romana earlier.

Their glowing, multi-faceted eyes surveyed the human intruders.

These humans, too, would become their victims.

'We have to be very careful, Adric. Do what I tell you, when I tell you, exactly as I tell you. Understood?'

'Understood.'

The Doctor considered the gap between themselves and the open doors of the TARDIS, and wondered how fast the spiders were capable of transporting themselves. He would find out soon enough.

He saw K9's body, to the right of the TARDIS. Spiders were clustered around and all over him. There was no sign of the head. Despite himself, the Doctor felt a surge of anguish. K9 had always been more than just a computer.

'Doctor?' Adric stooped to the floor next to Romana and, with more than a touch of apprehension, lifted the ugly carcass of the spider which had bitten her. 'It's dead.'

'Get it into the TARDIS, Adric. Take Romana with you.'

'What about you?'

'I'm going to fetch K9.'

Adric paled as he considered the number of spiders grouped around the remains of the Doctor's computer companion. 'You won't stand a chance!'

The Doctor seemed not to have heard him. 'You'll have to move quickly, Adric. As soon as we make a start for the TARDIS the spiders should head towards us. Ready?'

'Not in the slightest,' Adric answered.

'Good.'

Adric helped Romana to her feet, took a grip of her arm and

prepared himself for the Doctor's signal. He noted that Romana still seemed distant, somehow removed, but for the time being there were more pressing matters with which to concern himself.

'Now! Go, Adric!'

Adric sprinted for the TARDIS doors, dragging Romana with him. As the Doctor had predicted, the spiders started to move in. They travelled quickly on their eight legs, a seething, clattering mass of malevolence.

At the TARDIS doors, Romana stumbled and fell. Adric heaved her up with a burst of adrenalin-inspired strength, and hauled her into the TARDIS.

The Doctor had reached K9. With a number of swipes of his long burgundy scarf he sent the spiders which clung to the computer crashing to the cave floor, only to upright themselves and advance on their human assailant.

There were spiders crawling up the Doctor's legs, and it was a continuing effort to shake them loose before they could sink their venom-loaded fangs into him.

He clutched K9's body with both hands, one gripping tightly to the neck aperture, and lifted it up. Kicking the spiders away from around his feet, he started to make for the TARDIS.

He was almost there when a spider emerged from the neck aperture, crawling out onto his hand.

For an instant the Doctor knew total fear then, once again in control of himself, he swiped at the arachnoid, sending it scattering across the floor. Nimbly he ducked into the TARDIS, kicking away the last remaining spiders at his feet.

'Doors!' he shouted and Adric hit the control. The TARDIS doors swung closed. They were able to relax, secure once more within their Space/Time craft.

The Doctor settled K9 on the floor and turned his attention to Romana. She was leaning back against the console, looking inquisitively around the room.

'Are you all right, Romana?' he asked in concern.

'I'm fine,' Romana replied, then scowled at him.

'But who are you?' she asked.

8

'I am Beginning Surgery'

Nefred and Garif regarded the comatose form of the Marshchild with apprehensive wonder. It lay, as before, on the operating couch in Dexeter's Science Unit, the gills at its neck rippling gently, in time with its rising and falling chest.

Dexeter stood close at hand, nervous, waiting for their decision.

Nefred spoke almost to himself. 'In past ages,' he began, 'these creatures were regarded with superstitious awe. Figures symbolising the whole of life on this planet.' He paused for a moment, then swivelled his head towards Dexeter. 'As such, their origins were not to be looked into.'

'A wall of deliberate ignorance,' Dexeter snorted.

Garif interjected cautiously. 'Dexeter, what exactly do you hope to learn?'

'The nature of these creatures. We're afraid of them, we retreat from their presence, and yet we know nothing about them.'

'*You* know nothing,' Nefred firmly pointed out.

Dexeter became deferential. 'I was forgetting, Decider. I understood from Decider Draith that these creatures were mentioned in the System Files.'

Nefred studied the scientist in silence. Draith and Dexeter had been close friends for a long time. Had Draith disclosed more than he should have done to this man? Dexeter was in essence a good man, but in Nefred's opinion over-eager, a scientific zealot.

Dexeter went on even as Nefred played with these

thoughts. 'But, if we could put that secret knowledge of yours beside what I can discover ...'

Nefred cut in quickly. 'Your experiments would be secret?'

'Of course, Decider. If you so advise.'

Nefred took a deep, nervous breath, knowing he was now committing himself irrevocably to a dangerous course of action. 'You have my permission for the experiments to proceed.'

Dexter was almost delirious with delight. 'Excellent!' he cried.

'On one condition.'

'Oh?'

'We – the Deciders – are to supervise.' Nefred's glare chilled Dexter to the marrow. 'And there is to be complete secrecy. You understand?'

'I understand.'

Nefred turned away from the Marshchild. 'Make the necessary preparations, Dexter.'

'The creature's no good to us aneasthetised. The revival will take about an hour.'

'An hour, then,' said Nefred. 'Be ready. Now, Garif, you and I have to see to the Outlers. Login is with them in the Great Book Room.'

The TARDIS was in flight. The Doctor stood looking down at the controls, not seeing them, seeing instead Romana's face, the puzzled expression on it – she had genuinely not recognised him.

Now she was lying in her quarters in some kind of coma, Adric by her side. The coma had come quickly, without warning. At first Adric had thought her dead, but a quick check had confirmed she was still breathing, her vital functions barely discernible but nonetheless continuing to keep her alive.

The Doctor lifted his head, closed his eyes, and let out a slow heavy sigh. Opening his eyes, he saw K9's headless body standing in the corner. They had had no time to look for the head.

Thoughts of K9 reminded him again of Romana. He was

79

back where he had started, with his original worries.

There was no way of telling how long the coma would last. It had been Adric who had first pointed out the two tiny spider-bites on her cheek. Something in the spider bites. Not a toxin ... some kind of psychochemical.

The dead spider lay upturned on the console in front of him. Within its carcass might lie the answer, the Doctor considered.

Dexeter had a microscope in his Science Unit.

Refnal and Gulner had fully recovered from their ordeal by now, and had been shamefacedly reunited with Varsh, Tylos and Keara.

They stood in an incongruous huddle before the galleries of the Great Book Room, looked down upon by the Deciders, feeling very small.

Nefred began. 'When the starliner crashed upon this planet our ancestors vowed that their one endeavour would be to repair the ship and return to Terradon.'

'Each generation has renewed that vow,' Garif put in.

'The work is continuous,' said Nefred. 'On your behalf. Isn't that right, Decider Login?'

Login never took his eyes off his daughter. 'Yes. On behalf of all of us,' he concurred.

'Then what is to be done,' Garif wondered, 'with those that betray that vow, betray that work?'

'They are children,' Login argued.

'Very well,' said Nefred. 'And do these "children" now understand what we are doing for them?'

Garif. 'Do they understand the warning against Mistfall?'

Nefred again. 'And the supremacy of the community?'

Login. 'I believe they do.'

Nefred's strategy had worked. They had no time to waste on a group of maladjusted children – there were much more urgent matters, such as Dexeter's experiments on the Marshchild.

'Then let them rejoin the Preparation,' Nefred proclaimed. 'There is no punishment.'

The sudden materialisation of the TARDIS in the boarding area startled a maintenance crew of five who were working on a power-point by the door. They regarded the blue box speechlessly.

The doors opened and the Doctor emerged with Adric at his side.

'Romana will be perfectly all right in there, Adric,' the Doctor was saying. In his hand he carried a small cotton pouch, secured by a knotted cord at its neck. As they started off, the Doctor gave the maintenance crew a friendly wave and placed the pouch inside one of his coat pockets.

It contained the remains of the spider from the cave.

They gathered in anticipation: Nefred, Garif, Login. They stood in their galleries in the Great Book Room, turned to watch the wall behind them where a massive monitor screen – the screen which had once shown Yakob Lorenzil his first and only glimpse of the surface of the planet Alzarius – was lit with a view of Dexeter's Science Unit.

Dexeter was standing behind the Marshchild, wearing surgical garb, a scalpel held deftly in his gloved hand.

The Marshchild, strapped securely to the couch, was letting out low, weary sounds.

Dexeter, in the Science Unit, looked up at his own monitor and saw the faces of the three Deciders looking at him. It was a small camera in the wall above it which transmitted his picture to them.

'The anaesthetic has worn off and the creature is now fully sentient,' he began by way of explanation. 'I am about to begin a surgical examination of its brain.'

'We will be watching closely, Dexeter,' Nefred came back.

Dexeter lowered the scalpel, about to make the first incision in the Marshchild's skull.

He was a nanosecond away from making the incision when he heard a commotion in the Great Book Room. Looking up at the monitor, he saw the Doctor striding in through the Book Room's massive doors, Adric behind him.

'What's going on here?' the Doctor demanded, looking past the Deciders towards the screen, and realising in an instant exactly what was going on.

Dexeter smiled narrowly. 'Doctor. You're just in time.'

'Dexeter, you promised that you wouldn't harm that Marshchild!'

Dexeter assumed an anxious expression. How could he make the Doctor understand? 'Doctor, without a scientific understanding of these creatures, we'll be doomed to fear of them forever.'

'That's not scientific understanding, it's cold-blooded murder!' the Doctor retorted with vivid vehemence.

Unnoticed by anyone, the eyes of the Marshchild suddenly opened wide, staring and alert.

In her quarters in the TARDIS, Romana's eyes opened.

Dexeter was unsure. The scalpel wavered hesitantly in his hand. 'I – I repeat,' he said, without conviction. 'I am beginning surgery.'

'Dexeter!' the Doctor called out in a last attempt to make the man see reason. 'Stop! You've no right!'

Dexeter looked anxiously at the Doctor, then moved the scalpel to recommence the operation. He gasped as he found the Marshchild staring up at him.

Snarling furiously, it began twisting and turning underneath the straps, straining to break free of its restraints.

The Doctor understood what was happening. The Marshchild knew what Dexeter intended to do to it, and in order to survive was developing the animal strength in itself that would enable it to break free and destroy its assailant, to destroy Dexeter.

In that moment, the Doctor understood the Marshmen and their perspective.

'Dexeter!' he called out. 'Get out of there!'

But Dexeter was too afraid to move.

'Move yourself! Run!'

With a resounding snarl, the Marshchild erupted from the couch, its hands rising and finding Dexeter's throat. Relentlessly, those hands applied pressure.

The gathering in the Great Book Room knew they were absolutely powerless to help.

Dexeter put up a desperate but vain struggle, and soon he became limp in the Marshchild's grip. After making sure of the job, the Marshchild allowed his cadaver to fall to the floor, while it stood snarling, challenging the room with its defiant stance.

The Doctor felt a deep, despairing pity for the creature.

The Marshchild let out a reverberating scream and charged the work bench. With a single sweep of its arm it sent an entire array of sterilised surgical instruments crashing to the floor.

The creature started hammering with all its might on the surface of the bench, again and again just bringing both fists crashing down on it, faster and faster all the time.

The Doctor felt a surge of hope. 'It realises!' he said.

Nefred turned to him, curious. 'Realises what?'

'It's fighting the animal, it's fighting this new thing inside it. It doesn't want to act this way. Come on, you can do it ...'

And then the Marshchild went careering around the room, smashing everything within reach, shrieking horribly, cutting itself badly in its rage.

The room was a mess, with instrumentation lying scattered and broken all over the floor. In its centre stood the diminutive Marshchild, crouched, breathing heavily, head lowered, its snarls slowly, gradually, giving way to quiet melancholic whimpers. Blood dripped from the gashes in its arms. Quietly the creature watched itself bleed. The sounds it made were like a weeping child, but no tears spilled from its black eyes.

The Doctor was proud for the creature. It had won its battle with itself.

The Marshchild lifted its head and saw the Doctor's face on the monitor. Immediately it made a sound which was an obvious expression of delight, and started to hobble forward to the screen.

It lifted its bloody hands to the Doctor's face. It pressed ... but did not feel the face. There seemed to be something between itself and the Doctor. Grunting annoyedly, it pressed against this unseen barrier.

The smile vanished from the Doctor's face. 'No!' he called out. But the Marshchild was pushing still harder. 'No! Don't!'

The Marshchild drew a hand back and punched at the screen.

The glass screen shattered. The Marshchild's hand went straight through into the circuitry beyond. There was an explosion and a blinding blue flash. The Marshchild was picked up and thrown across the room. It was dead before it hit the floor.

On her bed, Romana screamed and convulsed, feeling a terrible pain running through her.

When the pain had gone she lay sprawled across the bed, head over the edge, mouth gaping, staring blindly into space. Unmoving.

.

9

'One Secret Our Ancestors Kept For Themselves'

The Great Book Room screen was knocked out in the same instant that the Marshchild died, displaying now only a hazy vista of electronic 'snow'. Nefred deactivated it and turned away. 'It can't have survived. Send someone to take away the bodies. We have to follow the procedures.'

'Procedures,' the Doctor muttered scornfully below them. 'Endless procedures, but nothing ever actually gets done. Adric?'

'Doctor?'

'Go to the TARDIS, stay with Romana. Let me know the moment you notice any change in her condition.'

'But you said ...' Adric stopped, sensing the Doctor's seriousness. 'Yes, of course.' He hurried out.

The Doctor waited for the doors to close behind his young friend, then turned, pointing a condemning, damning finger at the three Deciders. 'You!' he screamed. 'You "Deciders" allowed this to happen!'

The Deciders were openly stunned by this vociferous rebuke. Garif stammered, 'The marsh creatures are mindless brutes. Mere animals.'

'Mere?' queried the Doctor. 'Oh yes, animals are easy enough to destroy ... but have you ever tried creating one?'

'One might argue that Dexeter was over-zealous,' Garif suggested.

'*Not* an alibi, Decider!' the Doctor hollered. He subdued himself, with an effort. 'You three are supposed to be leaders.'

'Certainly, we are,' said Login. 'Of course, Nefred is now First Decider.'

'Then Nefred is responsible.'

'For the community, certainly,' Nefred agreed.

'For the *fraud*,' the Doctor corrected him.

'Fraud?' Garif shot Nefred an anxious look. Nefred returned an expression which told him to relax.

'What do you mean, fraud?' Login wanted to know, totally lost.

'Perhaps they haven't let you in on the secret yet, Login. Shall we tell him, gentlemen?'

'Frauds?' Garif whined. 'Secrets? What is all this nonsense?' He attempted a laugh and it came out as an unconvincing splutter.

'Perpetual maintenance,' the Doctor reflected. 'The same old tasks going round and round, the same old components being removed and replaced ...'

'No, Doctor,' Login cut in brusquely. 'You're too harsh. the preparations are necessary.'

'Preparations? Preparations for what?' The Doctor smirked. 'This starliner isn't going anywhere.'

'It – it must be made ready first,' Garif explained.

'Ready? Made *ready*?' The Doctor started towards the array of books immediately below the galleries. Just where he would expect to find located what he was looking for. Wrapping one end of his scarf around his fist, he shattered the glass front of the cabinet, reached in, and ripped the books from their places, throwing them onto the floor.

Reaching to the back of the cabinet, he wrenched out a flimsy, well-worn section of wooden panelling, and threw it after the books.

The Doctor regarded the back of the cabinet. He gave a knowing, humourless smile and stepped back, looking up to the Deciders.

Login leaned forward to enable himself to see the rear of the cabinet.

Neither Nefred nor Garif required to look to know what was there.

Login was startled to see, sitting at the back of the cabinet, a glittering, immaculate panel of intricate instrumentation, with read-out displays marked for altitude, thrust, telemetry and stellar proximity.

'This ship has been "made ready" for centuries,' the Doctor revealed to Login. 'It could take off in half an hour if you put your minds to it.'

Login, infuriated by this, a second of the Deciders' lies exposed, rounded on his colleagues. 'Is this true?' he demanded.

Nefred ignored him. 'You accuse us of wilful procrastination, Doctor?'

'Yes. The wilful procrastination of endless procedure.'

'But ... why?' Login asked. 'I don't understand.'

'Afraid to let go of the power structure you've created for yourselves here on Alzarius, perhaps?' the Doctor ventured. 'Am I warm?'

Despite the Doctor's revelation of their most well-kept secret – almost their most well-kept secret, Nefred thought to himself – Nefred managed to retain an air of dignity. 'You understand a great deal, Doctor.'

'Yes.'

'But not everything.'

'That's certainly true.'

Nefred waved an arm. 'We are standing in the Great Book Room. The galleries around you contain manuals on the repair and maintenance of every single item on this ship.'

'Everything is listed,' said Garif. 'Down to the smallest rivet.'

'Thanks to the manuals that have been passed down,' Nefred continued, 'we could take the starliner apart and put it together again perfectly.'

Garif hesitated. 'But there is one thing we can't do, Doctor. One secret our ancestors kept for themselves.'

Nefred looked the Doctor straight in the eye. 'Nobody knows how to pilot this ship.'

For a good few seconds there was total silence in the Great Book Room as both Login and the Doctor took in this staggering piece of information.

Vash, Tylos, Keara, Refnal and Gulner had been appointed as a maintenance crew under foreman Lazris Rok. They were equipped with manuals and with satchels of components, while Rok had their duty list, detailing the components which had to be replaced throughout their area of the starliner.

They came to a corridor junction and stopped by a wall power-point. Refnal and Gulner removed the power-point cover, Keara located the component from the instructions in her manual, Tylos removed the component and put it in his satchel, and Varsh replaced it with another, identical component from the supply in his own satchel. Refnal and Gulner replaced the cover and they moved on.

They had no way of knowing that the component they had just replaced had been renewed by another maintenance crew that very morning, and would be replaced again by yet another crew towards evening.

The Science Unit had been cleared up, and the Doctor was grateful for it. The equipment had been put back or, where something was broken, entirely replaced. It was one thing, the Doctor thought to himself, at which the citizens were very good – replacing things.

Login had watched with distaste as the Doctor produced the small pouch from his coat pocket, laid it down on the table, opened it and brought out the remains of the spider from the cave.

Now the Doctor was bending over the spider with a scalpel in his hand. He made one deep cut along the length of its underside and both he and Login were forced to turn their heads away from the malodorous fumes which drifted up to them from the creature's innards.

Lifting a pair of tweezers, the Doctor dug into the spider's insides and lifted out a smelly, steaming mush. Login was ready with a slide, onto which the Doctor placed his specimen.

'Now, let's take a look,' said the Doctor, placing the slide under Dexeter's microscope. He peered attentively into the eyepieces.

'The spiders only appear at Mistfall,' said Login. 'No one

has ever analysed one before.'

The Doctor seemed not to have heard, and was muttering away to himself. 'Leucine, Isoleucine, Methionine ... yes, there's the usual complement of amino-acids. This is oddly familiar. I've seen this cell shape somewhere before.' He lifted his head from the microscope, peering keenly at Login. 'What about Mistfall itself?'

Login was nonplussed by the question. 'Sorry? What?'

'Has anyone ever analysed that?'

Login became more than a little ill at ease. 'Well ... yes,' he began, 'but that is one of the secrets known only to the Deciders.'

'I suppose it would be too much to expect that that might be *one* secret of which you have been informed? Would it?'

'The information is privileged, Doctor. Yes, I have been informed about the Mistfall analyses, but ...' he hesitated. 'You understand, I couldn't –?'

'My dear chap, that's perfectly all right,' the Doctor assured him. 'Don't you worry at all.' He bent to the microscope again.

Login weakened, as the Doctor had suspected – had hoped – he would. 'Doctor ... every fifty years or so, another planet draws Alzarius slightly away from its sun. The cooling process ... it's inevitable.'

'Yes,' the Doctor mused. 'The mists ... and, you know, that would explain the bubbling in the rivers. An orbital shift like that is bound to cause a degree of seismic activity, releasing subterranean gaseous pockets. Yes.' He frowned into the microscope eyepieces. 'These spiders have an unusual amount of nitrogen in their cell structure.' He straightened. 'Mind you, it's not easy to judge – not knowing the norm for this planet. 'I'm going to need tissue samples from Dexeter and the Marshchild.' He froze, mention of Dexeter causing realisation to dawn. 'Of course! Now, where did Dexeter put that slide?'

He scuttled over to a nearby shelf, where he started going through a stack of slides and cultures, looking for what he wanted. He was still looking when the doors burst open and Adric rushed in, in a flurry.

'Doctor!'

'Not now, Adric.'

'Doctor, please, it's Romana!'

The Doctor stopped his search. 'What's happened?'

'She's gone – vanished!'

The Doctor stood framed in the doorway of Romana's room, Adric behind him. It took him a moment to register what he was seeing.

The room looked as though a typhoon had blown through it. Everything had been either thrown around or smashed or both.

As the Doctor moved among the debris, fingering some of the paraphernalia of the room, unpleasant associations with what the Marshchild had done to the Science Unit welled up in his mind.

There was no sign of Romana.

For a while they remained in silence, continuing to survey the destruction. Then Adric voiced their shared inner fear.

'Marshmen.'

'Marshmen?' The Doctor scanned the room with suspicious eyes. 'In my TARDIS?' He considered it for a moment, then turned on his heel and headed back out the door. 'Come on. Let's find her.'

Adric stooped to lift a small boater from the floor. Romana had told him while he was recuperating from his damaged knee that she had worn this during a recent visit she and the Doctor had made to Brighton, a community on a planet called Earth.

The hat was crumpled and torn.

'Adric!'

The Alzarian dropped the hat and hurried after the Doctor.

Romana came to a halt at the top of a flight of steps which led down into the vast, cavernous lower-deck area of the starliner. From the railing where she stood she could see across the entire, shadow-laden width of this most unused part of the great ship. Large emergency escape portals were spaced along one wall at intervals of some six hundred yards or so.

Something was banging on the hull.

Romana smiled, and in the darkness the pulsating blue veins which had developed on her face were starkly prominent.

The banging on the hull continued. Romana descended the steps – to greet her friends.

Romana had left something of a trail of debris behind her, various scattered items which the Doctor and Adric were able to follow through the ship's passageways.

The Doctor was a little put out to find one half of one of his very finest waistcoats lying on the floor of one passageway.

A short distance away they found another crumpled piece of cloth on the floor.

'The other half of my waistcoat,' said the Doctor solemnly. He saw Adric pick something up. 'What's that?'

Adric proffered his catch. 'The image translator.'

The Doctor examined it. It was badly damaged, a number of its wires bared, its central diffusion crystal fractured. 'No more pictures of Gallifrey, then,' he said with finality. Thrusting the useless object into Adric's hand, he turned and walked off. 'Come on.'

Adric shoved the image translator into his pocket and followed the Doctor.

The sign on the wall by the immense hatchway read: EMERGENCY ESCAPE – TO BE USED ONLY WHEN SHIP HAS ACHIEVED PLANETFALL. Romana barely noticed. With a wide smile on her face, she reached out with both hands to grip the door's wheel lock. At first it stubbornly refused to budge, having been out of use for some time, but even this area of the starliner had been maintained by the citizens, and after a determined effort Romana felt the wheel give.

In that instant, the banging on the hull stopped.

Romana turned the wheel through three revolutions.

The hatchway swung slowly open with a hum of power.

Beyond the entrance there was a thick wall of fog, ebbing, swirling, beckoning.

Romana stepped back, and waited.

Then they appeared, emerging slowly from the grey vapour, snarling quietly, ominously, heads twisting to and fro, assessing this new environment.

The Marshmen had at last achieved their objective. They were aboard the starliner.

10

'We've Come Full Circle'

They surged into the starliner, a wave of snarling bestiality, a number of the creatures wielding lengths of wood as weapons.

This was the group Romana had encountered in the cave. Their leader stopped next to Romana, staring at her.

She returned his gaze, unafraid – kindred.

The Marshleader lifted his hand. Romana pressed her own palm into his. Their hands caressed for a moment, and they shared one another's minds.

Releasing Romana's hand, the Marshleader moved off with the rest of the Marshmen.

Romana watched him go.

The Marshmen made their way up into the main body of the starliner, spilling out into the passageways in search of the humans.

Romana continued her task, moving along to the other escape hatchways, opening them, letting in the other Marshmen gathered outside the hull. They numbered in their hundreds, originating from marshes all over this continent of Alzarius.

Foreman Rok stood in the boarding area with his maintenance crew of Outlers, directing them as they opened the wall power-point by the door to fit yet another new component.

Varsh, standing at the back of the group, released a heavy sigh which drew a scornful look from Rok. Varsh didn't care. He was bored, and it didn't matter to him who knew it.

Suddenly his ears pricked up. Had he heard something?

Some small, shuffling movement? He turned his head, looking past the TARDIS, into the passageway beyond. He couldn't be sure, and yet ... He moved away from the others, across to the TARDIS, from where he could look right along the passageway.

Varsh felt his spine chill. A procession of Marshmen was heading straight down the passageway towards them.

Varsh staggered back towards the others. 'Marshmen!' he called hoarsely.

The others turned to him. Rok was flustered. 'Don't – don't be silly,' he began.

And then the Marshmen appeared from the passageway, pausing to assess the humans. Their chests rose and fell, their lungs rasped out swinish snorts.

'Gulnar, run!' Refnal shouted, breaking and running up the second passageway. Gulnar was right behind him. They ran as fast as they could.

Refnal was so frightened he didn't see the second group of Marshmen until he collided with them. Before either he or Gulnar could run off, the Marshmen's hands were at their throats, pressing, tearing.

In the boarding area, Varsh, Tylos, Keara and Rok heard the youngsters' death-screams reverberate eerily around the metal walls.

As both groups of Marshmen entered the boarding area *en masse*, the three remaining Outlers backed against the TARDIS for protection. Rok held back by the starliner door, hoping the youngsters might distract the Marshmen sufficiently for him to be able to make his escape.

'Varsh!' Keara screamed, flinching, arms raised pathetically over her face as the Marshmen advanced. Had the Doctor observed her, he might have considered the irony in that her stance almost exactly mimicked that of the Marshchild when faced with Omril and the other citizens earlier.

Varsh still carried his satchel. In a vain effort, he removed it and threw it at the nearest of the Marshmen. It did little to harm the creature, but the bag's contents – components of all kinds – spilled out across the floor.

Amazingly, the Marshmen seemed to lose interest in the

youngsters. They lowered themselves to the floor to examine these strange objects, intrigued by them, trying to deduce their functions. Varsh remembered what Romana had said about their intelligence.

Keara grabbed his arm and started to pull him with her towards one of the passageways. 'Varsh, come on, let's *go*!'

Varsh went with her. 'Move, Tylos!' He and Keara ran off.

But Tylos remained where he was, staring across at Rok. The foreman was cowering by the entranceway, one of the less inquisitive of the Marshmen towering malevolently over him. He was whimpering with fright.

For a moment Tylos was undecided, then he committed himself. He sprinted across to the entranceway, grabbed Rok's arm and pulled him out from in front of the Marshman. 'Run!' Tylos urged him.

Tylos watched as Rok made his dash for the safety of the passageways, and then the Marshman's arm closed around the young hero's neck. Tylos felt himself being bent backwards by the creature, hardly able to breathe, totally helpless.

Rok hesitated by the entrance to one of the passageways, considering Tylos's plight, his strong instinct for survival battling with his weak conscience.

Casting the youngster from his thoughts, he turned and ran from the boarding area just as fast as his legs could carry him.

'She could be anywhere.'

The Doctor made this observation as he and Adric came to a halt at yet another passageway junction, having well and truly lost the flimsy trail offered by the objects they had found scattered around the passageways. 'There must be a better way of doing it than this,' said the Doctor and, looking round, recognised the passageway designation notice on the wall next to him. They had been here before. 'We've come full circle,' he sighed, then walked on regardless. Adric followed.

'That's what the Decider said,' Adric piped up after a moment.

'Decider?'

'Decider Draith. At the marsh. His last words.'

The Doctor stopped dead. 'What words? Tell me what he said – exactly.'

'There's really not much to remember. He just said, "Tell Dexeter we've come full circle."'

'"Tell Dexeter we've come full circle"?' The Doctor reflected on this, then gave Adric a sideways look. 'How's your knee, by the way?'

'Oh, that was hours ago,' Adric said lightly, and lifted his knee. The Doctor frowned at the sight of the healed flesh through the tattered hole in the knee of the trousers.

'This is typical, is it?' he asked. 'Wounds healing at this speed?'

'Old people take a bit longer – sometimes a whole day.'

There was a gleam in the Doctor's eyes now. 'Rapid cellular adaptation – that settles it.'

'Settles what?'

'Back to the Science Unit.' The Doctor whirled round and headed back along the passageway at a brisk pace. Adric raced to catch up.

At the passageway junction, they stopped as the starliner's address system crackled into life. The Doctor recognised Login's voice.

'All citizens remain in your quarters. All citizens remain in your quarters. The starliner has been boarded by hostiles. Steps are being taken ...'

'Varsh!' Adric cried.

The Doctor turned to see Varsh and Keara running along the passageway towards them, out of breath.

'What's going on?' the Doctor wanted to know.

'It's the Marshmen!' Keara gasped.

Varsh was looking round. 'Wait – where's Tylos?' Suddenly aware that Tylos was most likely still trapped in the boarding area, he looked Keara in the eye and said, 'I'm going back.'

'No!' Keara begged, afraid for him.

'I'll see to Tylos,' said the Doctor, and he started to usher them off down another passageway. 'All of you take cover. In the Science Unit. Wait for me there.'

'Doctor, I want to come with –' Varsh began.

'In the Science Unit!'

Aware that the Doctor would not be swayed, the youngsters submitted, and started on their way to the Science Unit.

Steeling himself, the Doctor ran off in the direction of the boarding area, knowing, and fearing, what he could expect to meet there.

Nefred, Garif and Login were gathered in a nervous huddle in the middle of the floor of the Great Book Room.

After the instrumentation had reported the opening of the lower deck escapeways, reports had started coming in of Marshman activity all over the ship, and the indications were that more of the creatures were coming on board all the time. The citizens were in a terrified panic. Login's broadcasts had done little to restore much order.

'How did they get in?' Login demanded. 'The entrances were all sealed from the *inside*.'

'The Doctor has betrayed us,' was Garif's suggestion.

'I don't think so,' Nefred countered. 'The Doctor has already demonstrated his great wisdom. He is not a man to side with chaos.'

'Nevertheless,' Garif put in, 'chaos surrounds us.' He looked to Nefred. 'What are we to do?'

'Yes, Nefred,' said Login. 'What are we to do?'

Nefred considered. He turned, taking a few paces away from his fellow-Deciders, then swivelled round to face them again. He began, 'Login, you are a Decider now ... what *are* we to do?'

The Doctor approached the boarding area with the utmost caution, his twin hearts pounding rapidly. Apart from his palpitations, the only sound was the steady hum of the ship's power source – one of those sounds, the Doctor remarked to himself, of which you are always unaware until you become, through fear, sensitive to even the slightest disturbance of silence.

The Doctor emerged slowly from the passageway, his eyes searching every corner of the confined area. The Marshmen had gone. He allowed himself to relax just a little and moved further into the chamber. As he manoeuvred round the TARDIS, Tylos's body came into view. The youngster was sprawled on the floor, one leg tucked awkwardly under the other, very dead, his neck bruised and bloody.

The Doctor knelt beside the boy. They had never spoken, yet he felt a sense of real loss. The taking of life was always to be mourned, the taking of a young life even more so. The Doctor was puzzled to see that blue veins had developed on the youngster's face. The Marshmen must have been responsible. But how? Some contagious infection?

The low snarl came from immediately behind the Doctor. In one instant he had shot to his feet and spun round. He was face to face with the Marshleader. The creature was carrying his club. Perched on the end of it was the head of K9. The Marshman swayed threateningly, inching forward.

'Please don't hit me with that,' the Doctor grinned. 'It's irreplaceable.' The Doctor's blood chilled as other Marshmen appeared from the passageways. He was helplessly trapped. 'In – any case,' he went on nervously, 'you can't go barging around killing people. You see ... I think I understand now. I think I know why you're doing this.'

Amazingly, the Marshmen remained where they were. They appeared to be taking the Doctor's words to heart.

The Doctor was more than a little surprised that things were going so well, but decided to continue nonetheless. 'But, you know, there's really no need for this. So go on, go home. And take the others with you. What do you say?'

The Marshleader lowered his club. The Doctor immediately nipped forward and snatched K9's head away from the creature. The Marshleader snarled and backed further away, appearing cowed.

It was then that the Doctor became aware that the Marshmen were not actually looking at him, but at something behind him. He looked round. For a moment he was speechless ... and saddened. 'Romana?'

She stood at the entrance to one of the passageways, her expression enigmatic. The blue veins on her neck and face and on the backs of her hands pulsed horribly.

She moved ominously towards the Doctor.

Varsh was restless. He paced the Science Unit like a caged leopard, frustrated, eager to be doing something purposeful. He regarded the others. Adric seemed happy enough, fiddling with Dexeter's microscope on the workbench, while Keara was content to browse through a selection of manuals to pass the time.

'We're not helping much in here,' Varsh sighed. Keara looked at him, then turned back to the manuals. Adric appeared not to have heard. He was closely examining the base of the microscope, his attention taken by something there.

Varsh came up behind Adric. The younger boy looked up, almost suspiciously. Varsh lifted the slide which sat in the microscope, looked at it, snorted disinterestedly, replaced the slide and moved away.

Adric returned his attention to the microscope. There was a small catch at the base. Making sure neither Varsh nor Keara was watching him, he flicked the catch and a small hinged panel fell open, exposing the inner workings of the microscope.

Exposing an image translator in perfect working order.

Adric delved into his pockets, producing the Doctor's broken image translator. As quickly as he could, he removed the image translator from the microscope and inserted the TARDIS component in its place. He popped the stolen image translator into his pocket and sealed the microscope again.

Adric gave the image translator in his pocket a brief pat, smiled to himself, and moved away from the microscope.

This would be a pleasant surprise for the Doctor, he thought to himself.

The Doctor ducked and veered away from Romana's snarling lunges, all the time trying to reason with her. 'Look,' he said, 'you've got alien protein in your brain tissue. I've not had a chance to analyse it yet, but the effects are probably only temporary ...'

During all this the Marshmen watched on, silent yet attentive.

Romana lunged again and the Doctor nimbly side-stepped the swoop of her left arm.

'Please don't do that,' he said. 'Listen, this is your sort of problem. Psychopathology. Why are you doing this? Think about it.'

Romana attacked again. The Doctor almost slipped and fell as he ducked to avoid her grasp.

'Why attack me?' he asked. 'I'm the Doctor, Romana. The Doctor!'

Romana lunged forward with renewed vigour, and the Doctor brought his hands up to defend himself.

Romana suddenly stopped dead, transfixed by the sight of K9's head, held in the Doctor's hands.

The Doctor noticed this reaction, and saw a glimmer of hope for his companion. 'Yes,' he soothed, 'it's K9. You remember K9, Romana?'

There was a slight frown on Romana's forehead. Clearly, she did remember.

The Doctor reached out and stroked the doors of the TARDIS. 'And the TARDIS? Remember the TARDIS? Of course you do. The TARDIS, Romana ...' His voice had adopted a smooth, hypnotic quality which held Romana under its spell.

She approached the TARDIS, running her hands over it, old associations stirring dimly within her.

'Romana . . . I have some research to finish,' the Doctor cooed. 'I'll be in the Science Unit. Understand? You stay by the TARDIS ... the TARDIS ... stay by the TARDIS ...'

Slowly, he backed away, his eyes darting from Romana to the horde of Marshmen around him and back again. The Marshmen made no move to stop him as he slowly backed into the passageway and headed off, clutching K9's head close to his chest and thanking his luck.

The Marshmen moved towards the TARDIS, to join Romana in appreciating this peculiar object.

As they came near, Romana swiped at them, driving them

back, snarling at them, warning them by her actions that they should come no closer.

And indeed they held back.

There was a vast commotion of talk and movement in the Great Book Room. Login, Nefred and Garif stood in their galleries surrounded by stacks of manuals, leafing through them for information and advice. All around them, large numbers of citizens scuttled about, moving to and from the various book storage galleries, fetching new books to aid the Deciders.

Login was considering an engineering blueprint of the vessel. As former chief engineer he was best equipped to interpret the diagram. 'It might be possible to seal off the substructure,' he considered aloud.

'No,' said Garif, 'it seems they are already inside the main hull.'

'The bulkheads, then,' Login suggested.

'One recourse, certainly,' Nefred placated. He sounded less than convinced.

Login drew himself up to his full height, determined to have their attention and to decide on a course of action. 'Nefred. Garif.' They reluctantly turned to hear what he had to say, and he indicated areas on the blueprint before him. 'We must close these bulkheads, and these, and we must gather the citizens in here at once.'

'Yes, I can see the plan has some merit in it,' Garif muttered, already scuttling away to another area of the galleries to consider a fresh cluster of manuals gathered by the citizens.

'And we must do it quickly!' said Login, infuriated by his colleagues' indecisiveness. 'Are we *Deciders* or aren't we?'

'We must certainly respond to this crisis on a real-time basis, Decider Login,' Nefred placated, as though speaking to an over-eager child. 'But appropriately.'

Garif lifted his head from the manuals he had begun examining. 'Decider Nefred is right, Decider Login.'

Nefred went on, 'I have been consulting the histories of our relationship with the Marshmen.'

101

'While a single defensive response has a certain appeal,' said Garif absently, scurrying across to yet another area of the galleries, 'we must consider the long-term consequences.'

'It is not a defensive response,' Login affirmed.

Nefred ignored the remark. 'We need a holistic approach, I feel.'

Garif came forward, waving a short manual in his hand. 'I wonder, Decider Login, if you have had time to consult this manual on the peripheral unit power supplies ...?'

Login did not reply, did not see the point in replying. He stared at his two fellow-Deciders in mute astonishment, realising the awful truth – they were both frozen into indecision by the first real crisis of their lives. They were incapable of coping with a problem of this size.

Varsh had opened the Science Unit doors and was moving into the passageway outside when he felt a restraining hand on his arm.

'The Doctor told us to stay here,' Adric reminded him.

'But we're not doing anything,' Varsh retaliated.

Keara joined them in the doorway. 'What can we possibly do?'

'Just come on,' said Varsh, shrugging his arm free of Adric's grip and marching off quickly along the passageway.

Keara went after him.

Adric hesitated, torn between obeying the Doctor or following his instincts.

Instinct quickly won, and he hurried after Varsh and Keara.

Nefred read aloud from the manual laid out before him. '"... that the marsh creatures, though they rarely speak, are possessors of intellect. Furthermore, they have remarkable powers of adaptation to new situations ..."'

Garif spoke to Login. 'Their emergence from the marsh, for example. Breathing air through their gills.'

Nefred closed the manual and looked at Login. 'You see the difficulty.'

Login very nearly laughed, but within him he felt a

seething rage building up. 'You're suggesting we do nothing?'

'Nothing ... precipitate,' said Garif.

'Whatever measures we take,' Nefred pointed out, 'they will adjust to.'

Login allowed his tone of voice to become openly derisory, flouting the conventions of etiquette. 'So that is your conclusion from all this knowledge? From the entire store of knowledge in this chamber? Do *nothing*!'

Nefred remained dignified, with an effort. 'This knowledge – and more.'

'The System Files concur?' Garif inquired.

'They do,' said Nefred. 'Hasty action would only add to the general sense of panic.'

At that moment there was a loud crash from the direction of the Book Room doors. Everyone turned to see. The doors had been burst open, and now a swarm of Marshmen were spilling in through the doorway, roaring and snarling with hatred. With deadly ferocity, they charged towards the people of the starliner.

11

'We Cannot Return To Teradon'

'Evacuate!' Login cried.

The citizens scrambled for safety, pushing past and over one another to get away from the approaching Marshmen.

Even as they made for the gallery exitways, those exitways burst open and Marshmen tumbled out, falling on them, tearing and clawing at them. The cabinets were shattered, the manuals ripped from their places and thrown through the air.

As Nefred cowered in his gallery, manuals of all sorts rained down round about him, and looking at them he felt only a deep, deep remorse.

The Doctor ran through the passageways, holding K9's head close to him, wary that he did not run into a squad of Marshmen.

He heard movement up ahead, and immediately pressed himself against the wall.

From around the corner they appeared – Adric, Varsh and Keara.

The Doctor let out the breath he had been holding. 'I thought I told you three to stay put,' he said.

'We wanted to help,' Varsh explained.

'Doctor,' said Keara. 'Where's Tylos?'

The Doctor looked her straight in the eye. 'I'm sorry, Keara,' he said as gently as he could. 'Tylos is dead.'

Keara's face became expressionless. She blinked, and there was the glint of a tear in her eyes. She hardly heard the Doctor tell them he was taking them back to the Science Unit. Automatically, she followed after them.

Nefred saw the Marshman lumbering towards him, saw the creature raise the club it was carrying, and threw himself over the edge of his gallery to the gallery below. Behind him he heard the Marshman's club smashing against a cabinet, having missed his head by inches.

He was one gallery level from the floor, where Garif and Login were waiting for him, urging him down. Nefred started to climb over the edge of the gallery.

Suddenly a Marshman was beside him, roaring terribly. Nefred was shocked into immobility. Login and Garif reached up to grab Nefred's tunic, pulling him down. The Marshman's arm swung down in an arc, its claws tearing across Nefred's forehead as he was pulled clear. Nefred screamed.

Login and Garif supported Nefred between them and scurried away with him towards the doors. A number of citizens fell in behind them, leaving the Marshmen to continue their destruction of the chamber.

The Doctor stood at Dexter's workbench, rooting around among the bottles and instruments gathered there, Adric, Varsh and Keara gathered round him.

'Dexter hinted he was onto something,' the Doctor muttered. 'I didn't care for his methods, but he was certainly thorough.' He looked over his shoulder. 'Varsh. Lock that door. And Keara, help him barricade it.'

They moved instantly to carry out these instructions, dragging anything of size – including the operating couch – in front of the doors to keep them closed. The incident with the TARDIS had provided evidence of the Marshmen's strength.

'Presto!' The Doctor selected one small bottle from the cluster on the bench. 'Reverse transcriptase! I thought so. There's probably a centrifuge around here somewhere ...'

'Reverse transcriptase?' said Adric.

'Full circle,' said the Doctor. 'Ah.' He picked up a

centrifuge from off the top of a nearby cabinet, removing a number of phials from it and placing them in a test-tube rack. 'Dexeter,' said the Doctor, 'has been doing DNA analysis, Adric.'

'Good for him.'

The Doctor gave Adric a despairing look and switched on the microscope. Immediately the small hatch near the base burst open with a shower of sparks. The Doctor switched the device off, and investigated the hatch, withdrawing the broken TARDIS image translator and recognising it at once. 'Adric ...'

Adric already had the working image translator out of his pocket. The Doctor snatched it from him with ill grace. 'But it's what you wanted, isn't it?' said Adric. 'For the TARDIS?'

'Look, Adric,' the Doctor began, inserting the component into the microscope, 'other people's property ...' He tailed off, considering the small box of micro-technology. 'Yes, it would be useful. If this works in the TARDIS, it would definitely prove we're in E-Space.'

'E-Space?'

'The Exo-Space/Time continuum. Outside our own universe. I suspect what the TARDIS came through – look, do you mind if we do one thing at a time?' He snapped the image translator into place and switched on the microscope. 'Good. Now for a short course in cytogenetics. Gather round, everybody.'

In the lower deck area of the starliner, Nefred lay in the shadows, wheezing erratically, feeling his life slipping away from him. He could hear through dull ears the sounds of the escape hatchways being closed over, Login's voice loud and authoritative as he directed the citizens in their tasks.

Login is a very good man, Nefred thought to himself. One day, he will be a great man. He could hear Garif too, whimpering, complaining, panic-stricken. Garif should never have been made a Decider, Nefred considered. As an instructor of citizens he had excelled. As a Decider, he had proved useless.

As you yourself, Ragen Nefred, have proved useless, he told

106

himself. You call yourself First Decider. Yet when faced with a real crisis all you can do is hesitate, wait for others to lead your decisions.

Nefred was well aware that he was dying, and he was sorry that he would have no opportunity to redeem himself. He saw the blurred images of Login and Garif coming towards him, standing over him. He let out a long, wheezing, rattling cough and meekly gestured his fellow-Deciders closer.

In the background, the citizens watched on.

'Login ... Garif,' Nefred began. 'We have procrastinated too long. If you survive this ...' His words were lost in another coughing fit which chilled them all.

Login went down on one knee beside the dying man. 'Yes?'

'Seek out the Doctor,' Nefred ordered. 'He can teach you to fly the starliner. It is my wish that ... that you all ... leave Alzarius.'

'Return to Terradon?' Login asked.

'No,' Nefred retorted firmly. 'We cannot return to Terradon.'

Garif began, 'But if the Doctor shows us how –'

'We cannot return to Terradon.'

'Why not?' Login asked.

Nelfred turned his head to Login, and concentrated all his efforts to bring the man's face into focus. 'Because ... because we have never been there.'

His head lolled to one side, his eyes closed. Nefred was dead.

Garif gripped the corpse by the shoulders and shook it vigorously. 'What do we do?' he demanded. 'Tell us what to do!'

Login pulled Garif away from the body, saddened and appalled by the man's hysterical behaviour. 'Pull yourself together, Garif! He's told us what to do!'

Login started for the stairs, dragging Garif with him, and gestured for the citizens to follow them.

'We must find the Doctor!'

There was quiet activity in the Science Unit. In one corner, Varsh was preparing microscope slides for the Doctor. In another, Keara was watching over the whirring centrifuge. It contained a single test-tube filled with a few cc's of stark greenish liquid prepared by the Doctor.

At the workbench, Adric took notes at the Doctor's dictation. 'So,' he said, pointing to a couple of slides in front of him, 'you've got spider tissue, and the marsh creature ...'

Varsh stepped between them, handing the Doctor another of the slides he had been preparing. 'And here's the first slide of Batch Three.'

The Doctor accepted the slide and held it up to the blue lamp above their heads. 'Alas,' he said. 'Poor Dexeter. Reduced to a tangle of stained chromosomes.'

Behind them, the whirr of the centrifuge stopped. Keara lifted out the test-tube and passed it over to the Doctor. 'It's ready, Doctor.'

'Good,' said the Doctor, taking it. 'That should put Romana to rights.'

A cupboard which had been propped against the doors came crashing to the ground, making the youngsters start. Slowly, the shadows from the overhead lamp shifting across his face, the Doctor turned his head.

Bang. Bang. Bang. The blows fell time and again on the door. The barricade reverberated under the assault. The Marshmen had come to get them.

Adric and Varsh ran forward to add their strength to the barricade, but just as they reached the doors they burst open, sending the youngsters reeling back amid the tumbling equipment they had stacked up.

The Marshmen entered slowly, sucking in noisy, laborious breaths, their gleaming black eyes set on the humanoids before them.

'Adric. Varsh. Back here,' the Doctor ordered, and the youngsters came to his side.

'Don't let them touch you,' the Doctor instructed, surveying the creatures. There were three of them. It was enough. 'You understand? Avoid all contact.' Slowly he edged his way round the table. 'The rest of you, stay there.' Looking down, he saw a stack of oxygen cylinders lying at his feet. He snatched one up, then moved further across the room, the eyes of the Marshmen on him.

One by one, mimicking the Doctor, the Marshmen went to the pile of clyinders and lifted out their own. This done, they turned back to face the Doctor.

The Doctor's hand found the release valve on the cylinder. He turned it, and with an angry hiss a spray of oxygen shot out towards the Marshmen. They squealed, terrified, and backed away.

One of them twisted at the valve on the cylinder it carried. Over-zealously, for the valve came away and there was an eruption of oxygen straight into the creature's face. It hollered piercingly and sank to its knees, dropping the cylinder.

The Doctor turned his cylinder on the other two creatures. They shrieked, dropping their cylinders and backing away. A wide smile split the Doctor's face. 'It's the oxygen!' he cried. 'It's too rich – they can't adapt quickly enough!'

Immediately, Varsh, Adric and Keara leapt forward and snatched up cylinders for themselves. They turned them on the marsh creatures, herding them towards the doors.

The Marshmen, all three of them, backed away helplessly under the assault.

The Doctor placed his cylinder down and nipped over to the workbench. There was no time to lose. Leaving the youngsters to deal with the Marshmen, he inserted one of the slides into the microscope and bent over it.

He was unaware of the face which appeared suddenly behind the grill of a ventilation opening on the wall next to the bench – the face of Romana.

Her hands came up, grasped the grill, and ripped it free. Staring fixedly at the Doctor, she emerged from the ventilation opening. With the noise of the cylinders filling the room, he was still unaware of her presence.

Her hands rose threateningly, and she stalked towards the Doctor.

Keara was the first to see her. 'Doctor – look out!' she cried.

The Doctor jerked up from the microscope and saw Romana descending on him. 'Not again,' he sighed, backing away from her.

Adric leapt between the two of them, shooting a jet of

oxygen up towards Romana's face. She swiped at him, annoyed by the blast, but Adric avoided her attack and continued to direct the oxygen at her.

Romana's arms waved feebly, her eyes started to flutter. Without a sound, she collapsed on the floor.

Adric switched off his cylinder.

The Doctor patted the youngster on the back. 'Well guessed, Adric. Obviously her affinity with the Marshmen is more than just psychological.' He turned to Keara. 'Quick – the serum.'

Keara found it on the workbench and stood ready with it.

'Adric. Varsh,' said the Doctor. 'Go and find Login for me, and bring him here. It's very important. If you come across any Marshmen, use the cylinders on them. On you go, now, hurry.'

The two brothers started towards the doors. 'What if the Marshmen come back for you?' Varsh asked.

'We've plenty of oxygen here. Don't worry about us. On you go.'

'We'll be back as fast as we can!' Adric promised.

The two boys hesitated in the doorway, making sure the coast was clear, then sprinted away down the passageway.

'Now, Keara, the serum, if you please?' The Doctor held out his hand and Keara gave him the serum. He selected a hypodermic syringe from a tray of equipment attached to the operating couch, proceeded to fill it with the serum, then said, 'Now. Help me get Romana up here onto the couch, would you be so kind?'

Login led his small party of men along a totally silent, unsettlingly deserted passageway, gesturing them to caution and quiet.

At the corridor junction ahead of them they heard the roars of Marshmen. With urgent waves of his hand, Login directed the others to press themselves back against the wall. They held their breaths as the Marshmen appeared from around the corner.

There were two of them, staggering backwards, retreating from the oxygen being directed at them by Varsh and Adric.

110

Login's eyes lit up as he saw the youngsters. 'Adric!' he cried. 'What's happened to Keara?'

'She's safe, sir,' Adric assured him. 'She's with the Doctor in the Science Unit.'

'Can you take us to him?'

'Follow us. Come on, Varsh!'

They gave the Marshmen another burst of gas, then turned and hurried away along the passageway, Login, Garif and the citizens running with them.

Romana lay inert on the Science Unit's operating couch as the Doctor inserted the needle of the syringe into her left arm. Keara watched intently as the Doctor eased the emerald-coloured serum into her blood system.

'Suppose it doesn't work?' she asked.

The Doctor carefully withdrew the needle from Romana's arm. 'Then she's dead.'

The Doctor handed the syringe to Keara and she placed it on the tray next to the couch. 'Keara ... how long is it supposed to be since the starliner crashed?'

'Forty generations.'

'Forty generations. That's a good round figure.' The Doctor frowned and moved quickly across to the microscope. 'Can't be right, though.'

Keara crossed towards him. 'Why not?'

The Doctor bent over the microscope again. 'Evolution goes in quantum leaps,' he said. 'But it doesn't happen that fast.'

Keara frowned. 'What are you doing?'

'Karyotype comparisons. Analyses of the cell nuclei of these various specimens.' He stood aside to make way for her. To be polite, she bent towards the eyepieces.

Keara saw a microscopic view of the cell nucleus of the tissue specimen, the light and dark bands of the stained chromosomes showing up clearly.

The Doctor removed it, replaced it with another specimen. Keara could notice little or no difference.

'Definitely morphologically similar karyotypes, wouldn't you say?' he asked.

111

'Em ... yes,' said Keara uncertainly, stepping back from the microscope and allowing the Doctor in again.

'Of course,' the Doctor went on, effecting minute adjustments of the magnification, 'these inversions in bands eight to ten might be significant ... we need to establish how long the evolutionary process has taken.'

'From spiders to marsh creatures?'

'From spiders to marsh creatures ... and beyond.'

Before Keara could query the Doctor's cryptic remark, a figure moved between them and bent interestedly towards the microscope.

'You could try gel electrophoresis,' Romana suggested, lifting her head to smile widely at them. Quite her old self.

Silently, carefully, Adric and Varsh led Login and the others into the boarding area. At the sight of Tylos lying dead on the floor they halted. Varsh warned the others against touching the body, remembering the Doctor's theory about the infection carried by the Marshmen.

They started as a Marshman suddenly reared up from behind the TARDIS and lunged towards them.

'Run!' Varsh ordered, and as Login, Garif and the citizens ran off up the second passageway, he and Adric aimed their oxygen cylinders at the Marshmen and let loose a stream of oxygen.

The marsh creature recoiled, but for some reason it didn't seem quite so violently affected as the others they had come across. More likely, Adric reasoned, it *was* one of those Marshmen. The Doctor had explained about their adaptability. The thought shocked him. Could they already be developing an immunity?

Adric's cylinder spluttered and fell silent. He tried the valve again, to no avail. Checking the pressure gauge, he saw it read zero. 'Varsh – my cylinder's run out!'

'Then leave this to me – get the others back to the Doctor!'

'I can't leave you on your own.'

'Adric – don't argue, go!'

Adric realised that he had little option. Throwing his cylinder at the Marshman, he turned and sprinted up the passageway after Login and the others.

The Marshman swung its arms feebly towards Varsh, still daring to come no closer due to the oxygen.

Varsh became aware his cylinder felt lighter than before. He looked down at the pressure gauge.

It wavered just above the zero reading.

'*Forty* generations?' Romana queried, straightening from the microscope. 'More like four thousand, I'd say.'

'Since the starliner crashed?' said Keara, amazed.

The Doctor was standing behind them. 'Your Deciders have been procrastinating longer than we thought.'

'I don't understand,' said Keara. 'How can you tell all that from the marsh creature's cells?' She looked into the microscope.

'Not the marsh creature,' the Doctor corrected her. 'That's Dexeter.' He removed the slide and replaced it with another. 'That's the marsh creature.'

Keara scowled. There was no recognisable difference between the specimens. 'The same cells ...?' she pondered.

At that moment, Adric burst through the doors. He made straight for the stack of oxygen cylinders and snatched one up.

'Adric?' said the Doctor. 'What –?'

'Varsh needs help!' Adric cried, then turned and ran out, past Login and the others, who had just arrived in the doorway.

The Doctor, Keara and Romana ran after him. Telling Garif to wait with the citizens, Login ran to join them.

'Come on!' the Doctor cried.

12

'We're Trapped'

Varsh's oxygen cylinder was empty.

He tossed the useless metal cannister at the Marshman as it ventured towards him, then he turned and ran for the passageway. On the wall just inside the passageway, he found a wheel control. He turned it rapidly, and a fire safety panel started to descend from the ceiling, to seal the passageway off from the boarding area.

The panel came down slowly, and was only halfway towards the floor when Varsh felt the hand of the Marshman around his ankle. The creature pulled and Varsh crashed to the floor.

As the panel descended still further, the Marshman started to drag Varsh through.

The youngster clawed helplessly at the smooth metal floor, trying to struggle free. In vain. He could no nothing against the strength of the Marshman.

He heard running footsteps approaching, and looking up was amazed to see Adric racing urgently down the passageway towards him.

'Varsh!' Adric screamed. He dropped the cylinder he was carrying and threw himself forward onto the floor. His outstretched hand caught Varsh's, he tightened his grip and pulled. But the Marshman was too strong for him, and the panel was nearly closed. It would trap Varsh's arm any moment.

Varsh said, 'Goodbye, Adric!' and jerked his hand free.

'Varsh, no!' Adric saw his brother's hand vanish, and then the panel met the floor.

Adric heard the sounds of a scuffle behind the panel, the snarling of the Marshman, a stifled cry from Varsh ... then there was silence. He leaned forward, on his knees, against the panel, his cheek and hands pressed to the cold, harsh metal, and he started to cry for his brother.

The Doctor, Romana, Login and Keara found him like that when they arrived moments later. Romana consoled him while Keara operated the wheel lock, raising the panel to the ceiling again.

Login stood ready with Adric's oxygen cylinder, but it wasn't needed. The Marshman was gone. Varsh's body lay in front of the TARDIS.

Adric knelt beside his brother, more calm now, keeping the intolerable sadness inside him, wiping his reddened eyes clear. He heard the Doctor say something. Without making out his words, he knew it was a remark of consolation, of shared remorse. Yet within him he knew no one could share the remorse he felt. Not really.

A small hand touched his arm. He turned and looked at Keara. She was kneeling beside him. Her eyes were moist. Her lips trembled. No words were necessary.

The Doctor left them in their melancholy and inconspicuously drew Login aside. This was no time for becoming lost in sadness and regret. Time enough to count the costs of their experiences later – if they were still alive.

'Have you got any more oxygen?' the Doctor asked Login. 'Besides the supply in the Science Unit?'

'Certainly,' Login replied. 'We have an electrolytic power system.'

The Doctor was pleasantly surprised. 'What, you mean you actually make the stuff?'

'Yes.'

'Splendid. Enough to flood the whole starliner?'

'I'll see what can be done.' Login turned and hurried away along the passageway.

The Doctor and Romana stood back from the youngsters, watching them, but not intruding on their tragedy.

Keara untied the marshreed belt Varsh wore around his waist and handed it to Adric. 'Here, take this,' she said. 'Keep it for him.'

Adric accepted it, staring at it determinedly. Varsh had died to save their lives. He would always remember his brother – and so would everyone else. Adric smiled gently. Varsh would have been amused at his rapid elevation from outcast to hero. He secured the reed belt around his waist.

Login returned shortly, Garif accompanying him.

'All the oxygen valves are open, Doctor,' he announced.

'Let's hope it's not too late,' said the Doctor morosely.

'What do you mean?'

'Adric has described how the Marshman who ... the Marshman they met here reacted to the oxygen attack. They've already begun to adapt to the enriched air.'

'It might not kill them, then?' said Garif.

The Doctor was appalled. 'Kill them? I certainly hope not. But if we're lucky it'll drive them back to the marsh.'

'Shouldn't we open the doors, then?' asked Romana.

The Doctor smiled at her. 'Good point. Come on. The lower deck.'

Throughout the starliner, hordes of Marshmen were recoiling under the oxygen atmosphere which was building to a higher and higher level of purity all around them.

The creatures scurried, whining, along the passageways, towards the exits to the planet surface.

The Doctor, Romana, Login and Garif stood amid the lower deck area of the starliner. Groups of cowed marsh creatures were coming down the stairs and hurrying over to the escape hatchways.

The creatures had no time for the humanoids just now.

'Horrible,' said Garif. 'Quick, Doctor. Kill them. Kill them.'

The Doctor despaired of Garif's attitude. 'No, Garif. Look at them. You just might learn something.'

The creatures were pressed up against the hatchways, their hands clawing at them, searching for a way out.

116

One of the Marshmen separated from the others and began experimenting with one of the hatchway wheel locks.

'Look at their feet,' said the Doctor. 'The soles have flattened to allow better mobility over smooth terrain. When they emerged from the marshlands their feet had claws which enabled them to keep a firm grip on the marshbed. They're adapting fast. Given a little time they'd learn to breathe the air. Oh, they might wreck the ship first, and wipe out the crew, but the manuals in the Great Book Room would show them how to put it all together again.'

'They could learn to read?' said Garif.

'Oh, yes,' the Doctor answered. He considered the creatures. 'Just as they did once before, four thousand generations ago.'

Garif was dumbstruck.

Login spoke. 'Nefred's dying words – that's why we can't return to Terradon.'

The Doctor waved an arm towards the Marshmen. 'These, gentlemen, are your ancestors – almost come full circle. Look.'

As they watched, the Marshman who had been toying with the wheel lock slowly turned it, and the hatchway swung open.

Thick fog rolled in from the outside, and the Marshmen revelled in its caress. Quickly, they swarmed out of the ship.

'Romana,' said the Doctor. 'The other hatchways.'

'Right away, Doctor.' She hurried off to the nearest of the other hatchways.

'Nefred ... he *knew*,' Login breathed, stunned by the realisation. 'He must have learned from the System Files.'

'I remember,' said Garif, 'when I talked to him after he returned from the bio-data storage chamber. He seemed burdened. I took it for a passing malaise.'

'He was a good man,' said the Doctor. 'But, like most of you, a slave to the procedures.'

At the second escape hatchway, Romana picked her way among a group of wilting Marshmen and reached out for the wheel lock. She hesitated with hands outstretched, staring at the wheel lock with a peculiar feeling that ... a vague, stirring memory ... she dismissed the notion and turned the wheel. The Marshmen hurried out as the hatchway swung open. Immediately, Romana moved along to the next hatchway.

Back at the first hatchway, Garif watched the departing Marshmen with a growing feeling of revulsion. 'Our ancestors ... it's horrible.'

'Oh, I don't think so,' said the Doctor casually. 'We're all of us basically primeval slime with ideas above its station.'

'How can you compare us with those ...' he fell abruptly silent as a Marshman moved between them, staggering towards the hatchway. 'With those *things*?'

'Yes, I do see what you mean,' said the Doctor. 'They're adaptive, inquisitive, intelligent, and you people are just stuck in a rut. Still, it's your choice.'

Garif chose to ignore this rebuke. Looking round, he discovered that the last of the Marshmen seemed to have gone. 'Login, shut the hatchway.'

Login moved forward and spun the wheel lock. The hatch closed over.

The stench of the Marshmen hung clammily on the air despite the fact that they had by now all departed.

Garif watched the hatchway close with some satisfaction. 'They've gone.'

Login turned. 'But how long for?'

'What?'

'They've learned to get out ...' said Login.

'Quite,' said Garif, and then the idea that had struck Login occurred to him. 'But ... will they learn to come in?'

The Marshmen lined the banks of the marshlands, an army of them, numbering in their hundreds, joined in mental empathy.

The non-people of the metal city had won this battle, but there would be others, and the people of the marshlands, the *real* people of Alzarius, would be triumphant and crush the arrogant ones for ever.

The Marshmen opened their mouths and released a wailing sound that reverberated around the forestlands.

The Marshleader allowed himself to break away from the

118

empathy, and he turned his head in the direction of the starliner, recalling the mindshare with the off-world female. Her mind had understood their cause. The people of the marsh were not evil. They were not monsters, in the pursuit of destruction for its own sake.

The people of the marsh were frightened. They were aware of the threat posed by the non-people. Like, but unlike. Unchecked, one day to spread across Alzarius and smother the planet with their foul off-world technology.

On Alzarius, all should be nature. This was the philosophy of the people of the marsh. They existed to serve and to protect nature on this planet. They were the guardians of Alzarius, their lives dedicated to maintaining its purity from off-world corruption.

The non-people, they who had once been guardians themselves, had discarded this philosophy and had allowed the corruption of off-world to infect them.

One day they would remove their corruption.

The marshleader rejoined the mindshare with his fellows, and put the question to them: why does the maintaining of beauty always have to require the taking of lives? It is so very sad.

No mind could answer the question.

As one, the creatures entered the marshlands, sinking beneath its surface, disappearing under the murky slime – until it was as if no one had ever been there.

Adric hesitated by the doors of the TARDIS, looking anxiously around the boarding area, caught on the horns of a dilemma. He heard voices approaching and, not wanting to be discovered, nipped quickly inside the TARDIS, closing the doors behind him.

The Doctor, Romana, Login and Garif were approaching.

'So,' Login was saying, 'these first Marshmen came to resemble the original crew of the starliner?'

The Doctor nodded. 'The environment evolved the creatures most fitted to survive in it.'

'Terradonians,' said Garif. 'But we're not Terradonians.'

'No,' said the Doctor as they came to a halt in front of the

119

TARDIS. 'And you're not Marshmen either. Which is what they seem to resent.'

Romana frowned. A voice inside her seemed to be telling her that there was more to the Marshmen's cause than this, that she should explain this to her friends, but the voice was weak, a memory, no more. She decided to let it pass.

'I'm sure they'll return,' said Garif. 'If they re-enter the ship ...'

'We must do as Nefred said,' Login put forward determinedly. 'Doctor, you must fly us out of here.'

'Fly you? To Terradon?'

Login considered it for a moment, then shook his head. 'No. Not Terradon. But somewhere. Some other suitable planet.'

'Certainly,' said Garif. 'This is a colony-class ship. We could programme it to find a place.'

'Please, Doctor,' said Login.

Romana put in, 'Doctor, if they stay here, generations of evolution may be wiped out.'

'Please, Doctor,' Login repeated. 'It's our whole future.'

The Doctor grinned. 'All right. But just this once.'

Inside the TARDIS, Adric heaved a sigh of relief as he heard the small party heading off.

Moving away from the doors, he crossed to the console, looking over it carefully, at the central column, at all the alien instrumentation, at the innumerable lights which winked at him from their places on the console's various facets.

Adric reached into his pocket and pulled out the image translator from the Science Unit microscope. An image translator could always be replaced, he reflected, and in any case, the Doctor's need was greater. He placed the component down on the console and rested his hands on Varsh's marshreed belt.

He stared at the belt, recalling his brother. He allowed himself a smile of fond remembrance. In that moment, Adric made his decision. There was nothing left for him here – not any more. He wasn't leaving with the starliner.

Citizens milled about the Great Book Room, restoring

manuals to their places and repairing and replacing storage cabinets.

The Doctor, Romana and Login were standing in front of the flight panel below the Deciders' galleries.

Garif came hurrying through the doors, which were in the process of being repaired by a maintenance crew, carrying a thick manual. He seemed quite dizzy with excitement. 'Doctor, this is the flight manual – part of the supply held in bio-data storage under System File classification. I had it released to me.' Garif was now First Decider – the last. A new system of leadership was to be decided upon when they reached their new home – an elected leadership.

'The flight manual,' said Login. 'I've heard of it, but never seen it.'

The Doctor took the manual from Garif. The Decider explained, 'The pages referring to take-off were damaged in the crash.'

'Mangled by the first Marshmen, more likely,' the Doctor suggested as he flicked through its pages. 'Now, we can dispose of this in very short order. Watching?' He activated a sequence of buttons. 'Stabilisers ... power ... fuel ... thrusters one, two, three, four and five.'

'And the ground hold disengage,' said Romana, pointing to the appropriate switch.

The Doctor harrumphed and activated the switch. 'Yes, of course. Never forget the ground hold disengage. Goes without saying, really. And then, of course, it's simply ignition, which is that large green button there, gentlemen. See it? Good, good, good.' He handed the manual to Garif. 'Programming instructions are laid out very clearly. Shouldn't cause any problems. Have a good trip, gentlemen. Come along, Romana.' Immediately, the Doctor and Romana headed for the doors.

'But, Doctor ...' Garif spluttered.

'You want us to take off on our own?' said Login, dumbfounded.

'How can we?' said Garif. 'Such a momentous decision. Doctor, come back!'

The Doctor lifted his arm in a wave as he hurried out the

doors. 'The green button, gentlemen!'

Login and Garif felt very alone.

Login turned to his colleague. 'He's right.'

'I see his point,' said Garif. 'On the other hand ...'

Login guided Garif's hand to the flight panel. 'Garif, we must live up to our names. We must make this *decision* together.'

'Yes, of course,' Garif agreed.

The two of them stared at the green button.

'But you will agree,' said Garif, 'it does require some thought.'

The Doctor operated the TARDIS's spatial drive and the time column began rising and falling.

Nearby, Romana was crouched beside K9, completing the reconnection of his head. There appeared to be no problems with it.

The Doctor smiled slightly. 'They asked me to stay and be a Decider, you know.'

Romana smirked. 'You, a Decider?'

'I decided not to.' Smiling at his own joke, the Doctor removed his coat and scarf and hung them up on the hatstand.

Romana rose from K9, her work complete. 'Doctor ... what exactly happened while I was unconscious?'

The Doctor shrugged. 'Oh, Adric and I were far too busy to worry about you.'

Romana's eyes lighted on the small device perched on one of the facets of the console. 'Adric's left us a present, it seems,' she said, lifting it and handing it to the Doctor.

The Doctor scowled. 'An image translator! Look! he stole that ...' His disapproving frown slowly turned into a look of serious consideration. 'Still, still, it could come in very useful ... let me see.' He moved quickly to the scanner control and slid the image translator into place amid the instrumentation.

Romana turned the scanner control and they both watched as the scanner doors opened.

They saw a spatial vista, dotted with stars ... an image somehow tinted with an eerie greenness.

'It works,' said Romana.

'Unfortunately.'

Romana took his meaning. 'Negative co-ordinates?'

The Doctor nodded and let out a sigh. 'This settles it, Romana. We're out of our own space and time.'

Romana studied the scanner ... the green tint. 'Exo-Space!' she exclaimed.

'I'm afraid so. That thing we came through was a Charged Vacuum Emboitement.'

'A CVE.' Romana knew the term from her studies at the Academy on Gallifrey. 'That must be one of the rarest Space/Time events in the universe.'

'In any universe.'

Something else suddenly appeared on the screen. it shot past the TARDIS at incredible speed, streaking deeper into E-Space, propelled by a white-hot point of energy: the Starliner.

The Doctor smiled. 'They're out of their rut.'

'Yes,' said Romana. 'And we're trapped. Trapped in E-Space. Unless we can find another CVE. Right, K9?'

K9's head came up. 'Affirmative, mistress.'

Adric, standing on the other side of the control room's inner door, had heard every word they had said. He didn't understand much of it, but he knew that the Doctor and Romana were in serious trouble.

For the moment he would remain hidden – until the starliner was well away – then he would reveal himself.

Whatever lay ahead for the Doctor, Romana and K9, in E-Space or beyond, Adric was now very much a part of it.

'DOCTOR WHO'

TERRANCE DICKS
Doctor Who and The

0426200373	**Android Invasion**	90p

Doctor Who and the

| 0426201086 | **Androids of Tara** | 75p |

Doctor Who and The

| 0426201043 | **Armageddon Factor** | 85p |

IAN MARTER
Doctor Who and The Ark

| 0426116313 | **in Space** | 90p |

Doctor Who and The

| 0426116747 | **Brain of Morbius** | 95p |

TERRANCE DICKS
Doctor Who and The

| 0426117034 | **Claws of Axos** | 75p |

DAVID FISHER
Doctor Who and The

| 042620123X | **Creature from the Pit** | 90p |

BRIAN HAYLES
Doctor Who and The Curse

| 0426114981 | **of Peladon** | 75p |

GERRY DAVIS

| 0426114639 | **Doctor Who and The Cybermen** | 85p |

BARRY LETTS

| 0426113322 | **Doctor Who and The Daemons** | £1.50 |

DAVID WHITAKER

| 0426101103 | **Doctor Who and The Daleks** | 85p |

TERRANCE DICKS
Doctor Who and The Dalek

| 042611244X | **Invasion of Earth** | £1.25 |

Doctor Who and The Day

| 0426103807 | **of the Daleks** | 85p |

Prices are subject to alteration

'DOCTOR WHO'

	Doctor Who and The	
0426119657	**Deadly Assassin**	85p
	Doctor Who – Death to	
042620042X	**the Daleks**	£1.25
	Doctor Who and the	
0426200969	**Destiny of the Daleks**	90p
	IAN MARTER	
	Doctor Who and The	
0426201264	**Enemy of the World**	95p
	TERRANCE DICKS	
0426112792	**Doctor Who and The Giant Robot**	95p
	Doctor Who and The	
0426112601	**Genesis of the Daleks**	95p
	Doctor Who and The	
0426201310	**Horns of Nimon**	85p
	Doctor Who and The	
0426200098	**Horror of Fang Rock**	95p
	Doctor Who and The	
0426200934	**Invasion of Time**	95p
	Dr Who and The	
0426200543	**Invisible Enemy**	£1.25
	Doctor Who and The	
0426201485	**Keeper of Traken**	£1.25
	PHILIP HINCHCLIFFE	
	Doctor Who and The	
0426201256	**Keys of Marinus**	85p
	DAVID FISHER	
	Doctor Who and The Leisure	
0426201477	**Hive**	£1.25
	TERRANCE DICKS	
	Doctor Who and The	
0426110412	**Loch Ness Monster**	85p

Prices are subject to alteration

'DOCTOR WHO'

PHILIP HINCHCLIFFE
Doctor Who and The
0426118936   **Masque of Mandragora**   85p

TERRANCE DICKS
Doctor Who and The
0426201329   **Monster of Peladon**   85p

Doctor Who and The
0426116909   **Mutants**   £1.25

Doctor Who and The
0426201302   **Nightmare of Eden**   85p

Doctor Who and The
0426112520   **Planet of the Daleks**   £1.25

Doctor Who and The
042610997X   **Revenge of the Cybermen**   95p

Doctor Who and The
0426200616   **Robots of Death**   90p

IAN MARTER
Doctor Who and the Sontaren
0426200497   **Experiment**   £1.25

MALCOLM HULKE
Doctor Who and The
0426110331   **Space War**   85p

TERRANCE DICKS
Doctor Who and The
0426200993   **Stones of Blood**   95p

Doctor Who and The
0426119738   **Talons of Weng Chaing**   £1.25

GERRY DAVIS
Doctor Who and The
0426110684   **Tenth Planet**   85p

TERRANCE DICKS
Doctor Who and The
0426115007   **Terror of the Autons**   75p

Prices are subject to alteration

Prices are subject to alteration

STAR Books are obtainable from many booksellers and newsagents. If you have any difficulty please send purchase price plus postage on the scale below to:

Star Cash Sales
P.O. Box 11
Falmouth
Cornwall
OR
Star Book Service,
G.P.O. Box 29,
Douglas,
Isle of Man,
British Isles.

While every effort is made to keep prices low, it is sometimes necessary to increase prices at short notice. Star Books reserve the right to show new retail prices on covers which may differ from those advertised in the text or elsewhere.

Postage and Packing Rate

UK: 40p for the first book, 18p for the second book and 13p for each additional book ordered to a maximum charge of £1·49p. BFPO and EIRE: 40p for the first book, 18p for the second book, 13p per copy for the next 7 books, thereafter 7p per book. Overseas: 60p for the first book and 18p per copy for each additional book.